THE ENGLISH DRAGON BOOK 6

KATHI S. BARTON

This is a work of fiction. Names, characters, places, and incidents are products of the author's imagination or are used fictitiously and are not to be construed as real. Any resemblance to actual events, locations, organizations, or persons, living or dead, is entirely coincidental.

World Castle Publishing, LLC
Pensacola, Florida
Copyright © Kathi S. Barton 2019
Paperback ISBN: 9781950890057
eBook ISBN: 9781950890064
First Edition World Castle Publishing, LLC, May 20, 2019
http://www.worldcastlepublishing.com

Cover: Karen Fuller
Editor: Maxine Bringenberg

Chapter 1

Kip watched Dalton breathing. She was hooked up to a lot of monitors still, but she was doing very well now. Just seconds after he'd given her his blood, he thought for sure he'd been too late. Every single thing in the room had gone off like a testing zone for sound. Not only had he been afraid, but the nurse that had brought him in the room had shoved him back, then called for the crash cart.

It was over as quickly as it had started. Not only was the heart monitor going again, it was going at a steady beep, as well as a little faster. But her doctor assured everyone that it was normal, and they happily went back to their jobs. Christ, he was sure that he'd aged a hundred years in those few seconds.

Dalton still had the heart monitor on, and a few times over the last ten days it had gone off. Not because it had stopped, but because it had sped up in a way that had startled all of them. However, in between the fast and the really fast, she was doing well.

"Mr. Newton, I was wondering something." He'd gotten

to know her uncle Eric very well over the last few days. But it was her grandparents that he'd fallen in love with more. Charley, her grandda, was who he was sitting with today. "When you shift, what happens to yourself? I mean, you're still there, aren't you? Please don't think I'm being nosey. I just have never had the opportunity to have a straight forward conversation with a dragon before."

"I don't think that at all. And Charley, you've talked to a great many dragons over the last week." The man grinned hugely, and that made Kip smile too. "I'm still there. I can talk to my dragon, but I can't make him do anything if he feels his way will keep me, or anyone I love, safer. I want you to know that as soon as I gave Dalton my blood, you three became my family as well."

"Thank you for that. I started to call you young man, but I'm thinking that you're a great deal older than myself and my wife." Kip told them that he was, a great deal so, and left it at that. "Yes. My granddaughter, she means the world to us. Even before she was born, we didn't want to have much to do with the other two. I'm sure you'll meet them soon enough. I don't want to color your opinion of them, but I think we might have done that already."

"I have a few friends. You've met Kendrick and her husband Danburn. They have contacts in very high places." Charley nodded and said government. "No. Higher than even that. The queen of faeries, Kassian. She can keep tabs on people all over the world if need be. She's been keeping us updated on not only where the other two are, but also how close they're getting to us. Cassie and the others too. They have connections beyond what the government will ever be able to top."

"I'm glad to hear that." Charley looked over at Dalton and continued. "When she was no more than about four, her brother locked her in a closet. I found out about it later, when she was already out of it. He had it in his head that no one would miss her if he starved her to death. I suppose in a way he might have been right in relation to those at the house. No one cared for her there. I digress. She was locked in there for over a week. When Louis went to check on her, to see how weak she'd gotten, not only was she just fine, but she also knocked him on his butt with a ball bat that had been stored in there. You see, unbeknownst to her family, after the first time he'd done this to her, she began storing food in different areas of the house. Not only that, but water and something to use as a bathroom. Dalton, she learns fast. A hard lesson to be sure, but I think—I hope—it's what made her be able to survive what happened to her the other day."

Charley excused himself when he started sobbing again. He had been doing that a great deal, also saying he wished that he'd been there more for her when she'd needed someone. Kip looked at the young woman that he'd be spending the rest of his life with and moved his chair closer to her bed. Taking her hand into his, he kissed the back of it, careful of the IV, and told her what he knew so far about her family

"We have a good lead on this James person. I've not told your family as yet. I don't want them to feel like they've failed you more than they already think they have. He was hired by Luann. Cassie believes that she's taken out an insurance policy on you, and that they'll be able to collect as soon as you're dead." Kip wasn't alarmed when her hand squeezed his; she'd done this before. But he looked at her hand as he continued to speak to her. "We think that they'll be showing up any day now to see what happened in that you're not dead."

"I'm a good deal stronger than they think." He looked at Dalton when she spoke. It was only just above a whisper, but

7

he could hear her fine. "Where am I?"

"Ohio State Hospital. You've been here for a little over a week." She nodded, but still hadn't opened her eyes. "I'm supposed to let the staff know when you're awake. Do you want me to do that?"

"Not yet. I have a few questions of my own. Is Uncle Eric here?" He told her that he was, as well as her grandparents. "Do I know you? The reason I ask is, you're holding my hand like I do, and I feel strangely attracted to you."

He laughed. "You don't know me as yet. I'm Kip Newton. I gave you a little—well, a lot of my blood to save you." She said he wasn't human. "No, I'm not. Dragon."

She must have drifted off for a few minutes, but he had time to wait for her to wake again. When he was sure that she was out for a little while longer, he contacted Griff, his best friend of all the dragons that he loved.

Have you found out anything else about her family? Griff told him that the grandparents were broke more than he'd been told in the first place. *You mean they're more than just behind on a few payments on their credit cards?*

They're set to lose their home. Or were. Danburn took care of that for them today. I tried to do it myself, but he said that he didn't want them to stress any more than they already are. Kip said that he'd thank him later. *Also, this hotel is not something that they can afford. If I were you, I'd put them up in your house. Everything has been taken care of—and so you know, you don't want to ask. But the house is completely furnished, and all of Dalton's things have been moved in as well. The faeries needed something to do, and you were top on their list.*

I'll make sure that I put them out something sweet for this. If you could take care of the hotel for me, as well as take their things to my home, I'd be grateful. Anything else? He knew that there was. Griff would tell him too, but in his own way. *They're on their way. I kind of figured that out on my own. But what aren't you wanting to tell me?*

About fifteen years ago, your mate was in a car accident. No one has been able to put the blame on her siblings, but that is what the police are saying – off the record, of course. He asked him what had happened that made him mention it now. *Someone saved her. She shouldn't have been able to survive it – the accident had her running up under a semi's rear. By all rights, she should have lost her head. Not only was she all right, but she was awake and coherent. We were all wondering if you've had a taste of her. Just a little would tell you what sort of creature saved her.*

Hang on and I'll do that now. He didn't want to. Kip wanted to make sure she was going to be all right with him doing such a thing to her. But he also knew that if someone had saved her before this, he would need to not just thank them, but also find out why they'd done it. Closing his eyes, he licked the back of her hand that he was holding.

Kip, are you all right? He wasn't sure, and told Griff that. *I lost you there for a moment. It was almost as if you'd died or something.*

I'm processing. He was too. It was too much of her. Whatever had saved her had been very powerful, and had put a spell over her to keep her safe. They'd also shared a little of themselves with her, so Dalton had a great deal of magic. But only in the sense that it gave her a boost in protection and safety. *The best I can tell is it's either a faerie, a vampire, or both of them. I have no way of figuring out which.*

Christ. Kip felt the same way. When Dalton squeezed his hand, he looked at her, then to the bottom of the bed where she was looking.

I have to go. We have company. I'm betting that I'll have more information when I get back to you. Griff told him to make sure that he did. *Later.*

"Hello." The being, he wasn't sure what she was, seemed to be transparent. He wasn't sure that she was able to answer him when he spoke again. "You saved her. Both times, I would imagine. I wish to thank—"

"There is no need for that. I am only happy that she is with you now." Dalton asked the creature if it was safe to be around. "I am. I have no form except one that makes you comfortable to look at me. This, I thought, would be fine in that I showed you my true self. I am a—I guess you would call me friend. Dalton, you saved me once, a very long time ago."

He looked at Dalton, but he could see that she was confused. "I don't remember you. Perhaps, as you said, you were in a different form?" The being nodded and changed. "The lady down the street. The one that my brother terrorized a great deal. I was only at the right place at the right time, Miss Haggard. You were in trouble, and I was there to help you."

"Yes, but you were injured yourself, and did not let that stop you." She looked at him then. "Lord Newton, you should be aware that I have also made it so that your parents are delayed in coming here. A little magic here, a little there, and I have slowed them down to not arrive until you have dealt with the problem with the young lady's family."

"We're keeping tabs on them. They're on their way." She nodded and touched her fingers to Dalton's toe. He felt the magic that she'd given her, and could see a vast improvement in Dalton's health. "You enhanced her, and in turn, did the same to me."

"Yes. You are her mate, and in that, you would have received it as well even not touching her. I have no way of helping you any more, my dear friends. You will be as safe as you can be from now on. With the added magic that I have

10

given you, and you being a dragon, Lord Newton, there is very little that will be able to defeat you. That being said, you still must take care. The world needs you both."

With that, she was gone. Kip looked at Dalton, who was staring at the place where Miss Haggard had been. When he said her name, she looked at him finally. Asking if she was all right, she nodded, then shook her head.

"I would imagine that I could say the same for myself. When she said that you were hurt when you saved her, what happened?" She just stared at him, then laid her head back on the pillow. When she let out a long sigh, he thought that he could have gladly kissed her right then and there.

"You're my mate. Now, while I have no problem whatsoever with you being that, there are a few things that I should point out to you first. None of them are going to be anything that you can change, but you should know them all the same." He said that he could live with that. "Okay, first and foremost, you cannot make me do anything that I don't want to. Secondly, I don't know how to be a lady. I noticed that she called you lord. I'm assuming that means you have money and a title, correct?"

"Yes. So do you." She nodded and closed her eyes. "That's all? I mean, you only have two points. I can live with both of them, by the way. I want to point out that you have money because I do. Also, I've had some friends take care of your grandparents."

"What's wrong with them?" He told her when she sat up and glared at him. "I didn't know. I mean, I knew they were having a little bit of trouble—their words, not mine—but I didn't know they were that broke."

"They aren't. Not anymore." She nodded, lying back down. "You want more, or are you wanting to rest a little?"

"I want to rest. While I do feel better than I did, I'm still feeling off my feed." He didn't say anything as her eyes stayed closed longer each time she closed them. "Don't get too cozy in thinking that I'm always this laid back. I'm not."

"I never thought that you were."

When he was sure that she was resting again, he decided to find something to eat. Just as he was pulling on his jacket to leave her, Charley and Fern showed up with sandwiches and drinks. Kip figured it was time that he talked to them anyway.

~*~

Fern was glad for the new lease on life. Having things taken care of by the big man had been more than she'd ever thought to happen. Today he'd brought in a rocking chair so that she could sit with Dalton. It was the little things, she knew, that made her feel much better about Dalton and Kip.

"Did you know that I can hear you breathing hard? What is it, Grandma, that has you so worked up that you're about to rock a hole in the floor?" Fern got up and sat on the side of the bed with Dalton. "You look amazing."

"I feel that way too. Kipling, he helped us out, did you know that?" Dalton nodded. She didn't seem to be fighting off the drugs when she had a conversation as much as she had been before. "Your grandda, he's having lunch with the rest of the dragons to figure out what to do about Luann and Louis."

"You'd think they were twins, wouldn't you? I mean, who names their children such alike names?" They both laughed. "I talked to Kip last night when he was here. He told me that you were going to be living with us. Since I'm sure that I have no idea what that might entail, I'm very happy that he's taking care of you guys. You and Uncle Eric are all I have in the world right now."

"Luann took out a policy on you. What a thing to do. And

now she's all up in arms because she wasn't able to collect." Dalton asked her if she'd spoken to her. "No. But Kipling's friends, they're very informed. Louis was in jail. Did you know that? I didn't. but I guess he's going to be set free soon. I guess that the witness that they had somehow ended up getting killed. That is being looked into as well. These two.... I swear to you, Dalton, I have no idea how they are related to you."

"Me either. I guess they think that since I'm the black sheep of the family, they can do just about anything they wish to me." Fern told her about the family that she was mated to. "We're still working out the details about that, too. I'm not sure that I want someone in my life that can do the same to me as the other two are."

"I don't think you need to worry about him, honey. Kipling seems to me like a very nice man. I'm sure that as a dragon— Just listen to me. Talking about a dragon like it's nothing but a hound that came to wet on the front stoop."

"Where on earth did that comparison come from? Grandma, you've been hanging out with Grandda a lot since he retired, haven't you?" Fern told her that she wanted the man to get a job. "He's in his late seventies, and I'm pretty sure that he's sick of working."

"Yes, well, he could be a greeter or something. I need my peace and quiet sometimes." They laughed again, and Fern knew that she was only kidding. Charley had been her rock since the day she'd met him. "Enough about that. Tell me how you're really feeling."

"Like I need to get up out of this bed and run. I have been feeling like I'm only here for some kind of newspaper shit. I would really like something to do." Fern didn't point out that she'd been napping a great deal and must have needed the rest. But she also thought that she understood Dalton better than most would. She didn't need to run so much as she needed to be needed.

"I'm to understand that you have a job picking out the living room furniture for your new home." She made a sound that Fern was sure she'd gotten from some wild animal. "Didn't Kip ask you to have some input on the house that he purchased? I'm enjoying the hotel, but I have to tell you, Dalton, having a home is so much better. It's roots you can put down."

"I had roots, Grandma, and some dickweed came and fucked it all up for me." Fern didn't bother asking her to watch her language. She would, if asked, but it wouldn't last very long. Besides, Fern wasn't too happy with the events that had brought Dalton here either. "Where are my things? Hopefully someone had enough sense to put in a new door."

"I heard Kip talking to someone yesterday, and all your things have been packed up and taken to the new house." She started to complain, but Fern cut her off. "You have been hiding from Luann and Louis for years. Now that they've found you, I thought it was best that you moved again. I'm sure that they'll never get to you where you'll be living."

"That's another thing I don't like about any of this. I've had no say in what I wanted in anything." Fern watched her pout, something that Dalton rarely did. "I'm sorry. I was out, so that was just mean of me to say. But I'm out of sorts, Grandma. I need to do something productive."

Taking the little computer that Kip had brought in for Dalton, Fern brought up the pictures of the house that he'd taken them to see yesterday. It was a huge home, lovely too, with all the decorations for Christmas. Although Kip had explained how it had come to be his home, neither she nor Charley had objected to the way things looked — inside or out, as a matter of fact.

"Here. He said that if you don't cook then to skip the kitchen. It's lovely, by the way. I love all the new tile on the floor and the beautifully decorated back splash. Kip said that the faeries made it so you'd always feel like you were out of doors." Fern handed the tablet to Dalton. "I'd start with the dining area if I were you. There is a table in the room that was left behind, I believe he told me. As well as a desk that they couldn't remove from the home."

"There are built in china cabinets—did you see that?" Fern had, but looked at the pictures with her granddaughter. "Hardwood floors too. And the large doors leading out to the deck are great. Very open looking."

"The chairs are still being redone, he told us. I haven't anything to tell you about those." Dalton nodded and said she'd not change a thing in that room. Then she asked what the view might be out the doors. "There is a garden back there with bulbs, he thought. Also, there is a small pond that doesn't have any fish in it, but could should you want them. Not a koi pond, but a real pond to fish in. Your grandda is happy about that."

The next room that was in the grouping of pictures was the living room. Fern thought that Dalton's little couch looked out of place in the huge room, but she did enjoy the colors in it. There was also a fireplace in the room that took up nearly an entire wall.

"I would do this room in earth tones. It would be something to cozy up on the couch and watch a football game there." Fern could see that too. A fire going, a group of people over enjoying the game with you. "I was thinking that the room could use two couches, but I could be mistaking the size of the room."

"I was thinking that you could do one of those corner things. Do you know what I mean?" Dalton looked confused.

"I have since changed my mind anyway. But if you're going to go with only two couches, you should be aware that his friends come to each other's house often. And they're all big men. Like Kip."

"Would three couches fit in there, you think?" Fern nodded, and told her that she'd have room for a couple of recliners as well. "Yes, I think you might be right. I haven't any idea how wide the fireplace is, but if those bricks around the sucker are standard, it has to be a least ten feet wide."

"I do believe that is what he told us." She looked for the picture that Kip had had her ask Dalton about. "He wondered if you'd be all right with a large television here, over the mantle. He said that he has paintings in storage if you'd like to go that way, I guess. He said that he could put a TV in any room to watch games on."

"He watches football?" There was excitement there. Then Dalton looked at the pictures again. "I'm betting he watches things like a bunch of grass faeries, doesn't he?"

"No, I watch football. I played too, when — Well, I played it before too." Kip kissed her on the cheek then sat down, pulling out food from the large bag he'd carried in. "They said that if you'd like, we can go home tomorrow. That way you can have a nice look around the house before you decide on anything. However, because of all the to do about your being shot, we're going to have to make sure that no one knows that you're healed. Dalton, your grandda is coming up with drinks, and he said that you loved hot and spicy, so that's what I got you."

Fern loved this man. She wanted to think of him as her grandson, but knew that he was a great deal older than her. And Charley had been going to hang out with the men of the family more and more all the time. It was good for both of them for Charley to spend time with someone he could talk to.

Fern kept an eye on Dalton. She enjoyed the spicy sandwich, and like Kip, kept adding sriracha sauce to each bite. The smell of the dark red substance smelled too hot for her, but they were having fun outdoing each other, Fern thought.

After Charley asked her for the third time if she was ready to go, they left the couple there to deal with the clean-up. As soon as they were in the elevator, she asked him what was going on.

"He needs to talk to her about Luann and Louis. The morons are on their way here." She said that she knew that. "Yes, but they've purchased guns this time. It seems they're thinking about taking care of Dalton all on their own. Also, Eric has decided to retire from his job. He's looking for houses to be close to all of us."

"What does he have to say to her that he couldn't say when we're around?" Charley told her. "Oh. Well, I guess she would need to know some of that. The magic that he has, do you know how powerful he is? I mean, we both know with age comes more of it."

"He's very powerful. Danburn, the man we had dinner with last night? He's the king of all dragons, so he's like super powerful." There were faeries too that Fern had met. One of them, named Dot, had been with her every time she left the house. It was both nice and a little disconcerting to have someone right there that very few could see. "Fern, we—you and I—we should go out and have us a nice meal tonight. Celebrate, I guess. Dalton is in good hands. We're all paid up on our bills and house. I'd just like, this one time, to go out to eat and not have to look at the prices first. What do you say?"

She wanted to point out that they'd not been the ones that had paid off everything, but he was right too. They did need

17

a time to have a little fun like that. The two of them had been pinching their pennies until they about screamed at them. If she never ate another peanut butter and jelly sandwich again, she'd be fine with that.

"All right. Let's do it. But no more, Charley. I don't want us to get like this again." Charley said he didn't either. "Good. Let's go. I'm starved for someone to wait on me like I'm the queen of Sheba."

They were both laughing as they got into the long limo that had been there for their use. Whatever this man did for a living or had done, Kip was certainly taking very good care of them.

Chapter 2

"There is not one thing in the paper about her being killed, Louis. I had this sucker planned down to the minute. What does she think she's doing, killing my hit man?" Louis told his sister that he had no idea. In fact, he told her, he was sick of fucking hearing about it. "I don't give a shit what you are sick of hearing, you fucking shit. I paid for this to happen, and I want answers as to why it didn't."

"Because her balls were bigger than his? Her gun had more bullets in it? How the fuck should I know? I wasn't even in the same state when it happened. If you had asked me, which you did not, then I would have told you that robbing a bank, like I wanted to do, would have been safer and quicker than trying to kill her again. And with money, we could have gotten a better hit man." He stood up and walked around the tiny house his sister was renting. "Besides, with him dead, you didn't have to pay him off anyway, if you want to think about it that way."

"I guess you're right about that." He nodded. If she was keeping score, which she rarely did if it wasn't in her favor, he was ahead by six points since he'd gotten out of jail. "What is

19

it you have to do now that you're set free again?"

"Behave. They say that to me every time, as if that is going to keep me from trying something new. I mean, what is the point of living if you can't live the way you want to?" Louis didn't expect her to have an answer, so wasn't disappointed when she only walked to the couch where he'd been sitting. "What are your big plans for taking out our baby sister?"

"I don't have any right now. I thought for sure this thing with James was a sure thing. Damn it! Why doesn't she just take the hit and die for us?"

Louis was no longer sure why she had to be dead. It wasn't as if he had anything that he could honestly point at Dalton about and blame directly on her. Other than she had money, that was. Dalton, for the most part, had left them alone.

There was really no need for them to try and get money from her either. They had both inherited the house and the money. He had a car to drive around, as did Luann. Money was there should they want it. Not as much as they wanted, but it was there. The house had been paid off, the taxes kept up for another ten years. The furniture had been nice and comfy. Nothing about their parents' dying had put them in dire straits, but the death of Dalton would make their lives better.

They had sold the house for a considerable amount of money. The furniture as well. There were stocks that they'd cashed out, and insurance. There had been a delay in getting things from the estate. The police, as well as the insurance company, were sure that they'd killed their parents.

There wasn't any proof of it—nothing that they could pin on either of them. It had taken Louis a week to keep Luann from trying to blame it on Dalton. He'd been sure that as soon as she opened her mouth to do that, they'd hold everything up for that much longer.

"You do know that it was easier to kill off Mom and Dad than it is for us to kill Dalton. Cheaper too." Louis said that it had been, but their parents had been stupid and he didn't think that Dalton was. "You never thought she was stupid. I wonder why that is?"

"Well, for starters, she graduated from high school about a month before she turned twelve. An entire year before you did, as a matter of fact. Then there was the added knowledge that she had about a million bucks in her accounts even after she got out of college." Louis was sure that she'd been a hit man in college, but he could never prove it. "Then there is the fact that she not only has money, but she seems to do what she wants when she wants to."

"We can do what we want when we want." Louis just stared at her. "Okay, we can't, but I get my hair done once a week, and my nails too when I need to. I doubt very much if Dalton has ever been in a beauty parlor, much less even had her nails buffed. You have never been without a goodly amount of money in your pocket when you're out."

"Why do you want her dead, is my question?" Luann said that she hated her. "Why? I'm not saying that you're right or wrong in your answer, Luann, but why are you spending money that you really don't have on killing off Dalton, when she's done nothing to us?"

"She's breathing, isn't she? Does this mean that you're not going to celebrate with me when I do get her dead?" Louis said that he would even help her with this, but he was curious why it was her number one thing of late. "Did I tell you that I found out why she has bucks? It's all lottery winnings. Every dollar of it that she's not made at her job, it's from winnings. What the fuck is she doing that makes her so lucky at that shit?"

He didn't know. Louis refrained from telling her that

21

he'd hit a nice sized winning just that morning. Five grand. He thought that he might live longer by keeping quiet. As she went on and on about Dalton and her incredible luck, he picked up the newspaper and scanned the headlines for something to take his mind off of Luann. She was becoming such a bore lately, and he was going to have to find himself better digs, at least quieter ones, if he didn't want to have to go back to jail. Not for murdering Dalton, but Luann.

"What the hell is that?" He looked at Luann, wondering what had set her on him now. "Louis, it says that she's getting married. To a multi billionaire. When the hell did that happen?" He turned the paper around, but Luann snatched it out of his hands. "Mother fuck. This has to be a misprint. There isn't any way that she has that kind of luck."

He took the paper back and began reading about his sister. Dalton really had hit the big times with this. Lord Kipling Newton, Duke of Winehammer Castle, was set to marry Dalton Mueller of Ohio in two weeks. Louis read out loud where they'd be residing, and what sort of things that they were having done to their home.

"Do you suppose that he shits gold bars too? I've heard you say that about Dalton enough." He turned to look at Luann when she didn't answer. The glass bottle hit him square between the eyes and knocked him out for a second. "What the fuck was that for?"

Louis knew better than to hit his sister back. She would kill him. That wasn't a figure of speech either. She would pull out a gun from someplace on her person and blow his fucking head off. Standing up, he asked her again what she'd been thinking.

"That you should know better by now than to piss me off." Louis pointed out that he'd not written the article. Not even contributed anything to it. "You are acting like this is something special. That you're proud of little lost Dalton in this."

"What the fuck are you talking about? I was reading the— You know what, I don't care. You call me when you're in a better mood. I'm imagining that will be sometime in the long away future." He was out the door and in his car before he could get hit again. "Christ, she's a basket case."

As he drove around the town, he decided to catch a flight to Ohio. It wouldn't be that far, he surmised. A few hours on a plane. Louis knew that he could drive, but he didn't like to be on the highway, and people pissed him off if he had to sit close to them. But this would be so much quicker, and he was all for that right now. Booking the flight, he thought about Luann. Fuck her, she could make her own rules concerning Dalton.

After less than an hour in the air, he was landing in Columbus. The last he'd heard about Dalton she was in the big hospital there. Thinking about going to visit his grandparents to hit them up for a hotel room, he had to smile about that. They'd rather pay for a hotel room than to allow him in their home. Louis could have paid for the room himself, but his motto was, why pay for what someone else is willing to fork out money for? It was why he went to weddings uninvited, crashed the open buffets of his friends, and shared rides whenever he could. He had money, but he was also a cheap bastard.

The house was for sale, he noticed. Not only that, but someone had not just trimmed the tree out front, but they'd shoveled the driveway and put in a new mailbox. Parking in the driveway, he got out of his car to have a look around.

Pulling out his cell when he realized that the house was completely devoid of anything, Louis called the real estate office advertised on the front lawn. He told her who he was.

"I was just wondering about the house for sale. It was my grandparents', and I don't know where they've moved to. Has something happened to them?" The man on the other end asked him to hang on a moment. "Sure. Whatever it takes to get to the bottom of this. I had no idea that they were selling."

Louis was put on hold and he waited. Since it was cold as hell, he got back into his car to wait. It seemed several times that he'd been hung up on, but once another man came on the line, Louis felt himself straighten up and feel underdressed. And all the man had done was say his name.

"Mr. Mueller, I presume." He said that he was, his back hurting for trying his best to make it stiffer. "My name is Lord Newton. May I ask what concern it is that your grandparents are selling their home? Last time you had any contact with them was over four years ago, when you tried to have your sister, Dalton, my future wife, killed in an automobile accident."

"I didn't have anything— What do you mean, your future wife? And they're my grandparents. I have every right to know what they're doing with my inheritance." Louis didn't know why he'd said that last bit. His balls were now clogging his throat, he was so nervous. "Why did they transfer me to you anyway? You're not related to us. Even if you think you're marrying my sister, you have no right to question me about anything I do."

"I now own the house that they were living in. I also hold the note on your other sister's home. And as of an hour ago, I bought up all the debt that Luann owes to nearly every bookie in your town. There is also the matter of your debts. Not nearly as big as Ms. Mueller's, but they are now mine to call for whenever I wish. I did not, however, pay off the hit man that she's hired, nor have I paid the money to the family of the man that my future wife was nearly killed by. Those, I think, should be paid for by your conniving sister, Luann. The money you have on you now, all one hundred and twelve dollars, is all that you'll have for some time now. So if I were you, I'd take care not to spend it on the new shoes you were looking at while on the plane to get to Ohio."

Turning off the heater in his car, Louis opened the window a little. He was suddenly very hot. Not only that, but he felt as if the man was right there with him. He seemed to know every little misdeed that he and Luann had done.

"Do you have someone watching us? Spying on the two of us?" He simply said yes, as if it were no big deal to do that. "You have balls, I'll tell you that, buddy. I don't know what you think you're going to gain by buying up the things we owe, but good luck trying to get anything from either of us. My sister there, your *future wife*, she should have told you that we don't take lightly to threats, and we're meaner than she'll ever be."

"You think so, do you? And like you, I've decided that having an insurance policy on both you and Luann is very helpful. But the ones that I have on you two will pay off. Because if you fuck around with me, you're going to be dead." Swallowing hard, Louis, trying to sound braver than he was feeling, asked him if he was threatening him. "Of course I'm not. I'm telling you the truth. You come near my family — that would include Eric and the grandparents and Dalton — and I will collect. One way or the other, you can bet I'm going to kill you in the slowest way I can possibly think of. And when I'm finished, you'll not be recognizable by anyone. Not unless there is dental work used."

The tone on his phone had him ending the call. The dial tone, he supposed, was loud in the little car. Looking around, trying to see if he really did have someone watching him, Louis screamed when the phone rang. It was his sister.

"What the fuck do you want?" He was testy, and knew that the only way he would be able to get by with it was because they were miles apart. Luann asked him where he was. "I'm sitting in my car at the grandparents' house. Christ, Luann. I just spoke with—"

Luann cut him off, screaming at him for not telling her where he was going. Closing the phone, Louis decided that he'd had enough people talking to him today. He was going to find a hotel, sleep it off, and get the fuck out of there first thing in the morning. Fuck this shit, he thought. I'm not hanging around here anymore.

~*~

Dalton had been sitting on the couch that she liked for the last hour. She didn't look around, didn't speak, and she certainly wasn't going to touch the tea glass that was sitting beside her until her mind was back where it should have been. Mostly out of la-la land.

"Are you listening to me?" Shaking her head, she heard Kip laugh but didn't look up. It was tempting to just smack him, but she'd have to look up and she wasn't ready for that just yet. "What part of this is freaking you out? The house? The faeries? Or is it me?"

"All of the above. Don't talk to me yet. I'm still working this around in my head." He stretched out his long legs and she could see his shoes. Tennis shoes that looked like they'd seen better days. "What are you doing with nasty shoes on in this house? Do you want to ruin the carpet?"

"There is no carpet in this part of the house. And my shoes are not nasty, they're well worn. I was burning out the mess my parents left me at the castle." She looked at him and asked him if he really had a castle. "I do. It's cooling down right now, but I'll take you there when you can walk on the floors without burning your feet."

26

"You're serious." Kip nodded. "Why is it—? I'm not sure I want to ask you anything at the moment, but I would like to know why your home is cooling off. Not to mention, how long it will take to cool off."

"It's cooling off because I used my dragon to burn out the mess that my parents left, as I said twice now. You're not listening to me very well." Dalton flipped him off. All it did was make him laugh more. "Dragons' breath is very warm, hotter than anything here on this earth. The stone, it was forged by dragons, my grandparents, a very long time ago, so it won't be harmed by it. However, it will hold the heat for a season or two. It won't take as long now because it has the winter months to cool it down faster."

"So, what you're telling me is that I'll never see the castle filled like it used to be. At least not on the inside." He said she could see it now, but even the grounds were not cleaned up. "Don't be an ass. I'm not going to live for another two seasons the way my family is going."

"I spoke to them too, today." She asked him why he'd do that. "Your brother wanted to know why your grandparents' home has a for sale sign in front of it. I took that opportunity to let him know that I won't tolerate him coming around you anymore. Any of the people currently living here."

She made the mistake of looking around again. There were so many little people in the room with them, all of them waiting. Dalton knew all she had to do was to nod or something that she liked the couch. Looking back at Kip, she felt reasonably better about it.

"I don't understand a lot of things going on. I'm not a wimp or anything like that, but I'm certainly overwhelmed right now." Kip told her that was understandable. "Can I just, I don't know, ask questions as they slow down enough for me to put to words? You know, ease me into the insane asylum?"

27

"You're not crazy." Dalton asked him to prove it. He asked her three questions, ones that she would have to know the answers to. "See, not crazy. I would like to tell you, Dalton. If you were to let one of them peek into your mind to see what you've ever thought of as a lovely home, they'll leave us alone when they're done."

"For how long?" He told her that she could dismiss them all now if she wanted. But they'd be back. "So, they're really here? All these tiny people are really in your house, and waiting on me to make a decision so that they can finish up your home?"

"Our home, but yes, that's what they're wanting to do for you." She shook her head and looked at the group of tiny creatures. One of them came to sit on her knee, and Dalton had a moment of panic. "They would die for you, Dalton. The same as they would for any of us. Her name is Button. Button is in charge of this home. She can do whatever you want at any time you wish. You only have to allow her to touch your skin, and she'll be able to make this house your dream come true."

She watched as Button sat down on her leg. It was then that she noticed that she had tennis shoes on and not pointy shoes. Laughing at the stupidity of her thought, Dalton put out her hand. Button stepped onto her palm without touching any part of her flesh. Then, shakily, she took her hand to her face with Button still on her palm.

"What if I told you that I have no idea what I wanted in a home? That I'd never thought of finding a husband. For that matter, cared if I did or not. That having a home, lovely or not, hasn't been anything that I've given any thought to." Button moved closer to her nose so that she could see that her eyes matched the sparkly outfit that she had on. "You're very bright, aren't you?"

"Would it make you feel better if I were just normal?" Button's outfit disappeared and she was in a pair of jeans and an old T-shirt. The shoes stayed. "I can't make you less overwhelmed, my lady. But I can ease you into your home by making it something that you're proud of. Also a place that you can feel less stressed, a place you can rest your mind and ease your heart. Let us start with colors. You enjoy the outdoors, do you not?"

"I love earth tones, yes. Greens of every color is something that I have in my bedroom—had in my bedroom." Button nodded. Then she asked if she could touch her. "You may, but I don't want you disappointed when you find nothing more than a squad room for reference."

"You could never disappoint me, my lady. You are here now, and Lord Kip is very happy. Why, I heard him whistling the other day. It was quite badly done, but he was trying." Dalton laughed and felt better for it. "You allow me to find what I can, and we all will serve you in any way that we can with your home."

The touch, while slight, was powerful. Magic was there, but it wasn't intrusive, nor did it hurt. As Button seemed to be concentrating on what she was looking for, Dalton thought of all the homes that she'd been in. The ones that she'd found people who had been killed or injured in.

"I do not wish to give you white tape on the floor, my lady. Perhaps you can think of something cheerier." That, too, made her laugh, and she thought of her grandmother's home. "Much nicer. I can work with this. It is comfort that you seek when you visit this home."

"It is. And love. I don't have a great deal of that in my life. Not even as a child." She thought of her grandparents. "They had a lake behind their home. It had a dock that floated in the middle of it. That's how I learned to swim. My brother

29

had pushed me in, and had it not been for my grandmother coming in for me, I might well have drowned."

"He is a bad person." Dalton nodded and closed her eyes now. "You loved the home for the comfort, but it is more than that, isn't it? It was a place you could go and be safe. Safety for you was something you had to find rather than having it at home."

"Yes." Dalton looked at Kip when he took her other hand. "I'm a person who puts on a big front, lets people think that I'm bad assed. But inside I'm a mess of fear, turmoil, and insecurities. I hate feeling that way all the time, so I hide it by pushing people away, no matter who they say they are to me. I take on jobs that are dangerous so that I can prove to those around me that I'm not afraid of anything. But I am."

"I'll protect you when you want me to." Dalton didn't know if he would or not. She'd been disappointed by people who should have protected her and didn't. Dalton told Kip that. "I will never lie to you, Dalton. I won't ever hit you or harm you in any way, by word or violence. You have my word that I will love you forever. My forever, yours now too. You own my heart, my soul, and my body. Everything that I have, now and in the future, is yours. All that you have, it is yours. I want nothing from you that you are not willing to give me. I would never ask you to do something that you aren't wholly willing to do. I will— I swear on my dragon that I will forever hold you near and dear to me. Forevermore."

"That sounded like a wedding promise." He said that it was. His to her. "You just married me? That's not possible. I don't even know that I could ever love you."

"A dragon, unlike any other creatures, does not have to bond with his mate through sex or the exchange of fluids. The moment that I knew what you were to me, the very moment that I could smell on your skin the scent that only I can smell, I

30

knew that you were meant only for me." She asked him about the blood that he'd given her. "That was to save your life. I knew what you were to me before I did that. I would have done that to save you no matter if you were my mate or not. To be able to save a beautiful creature such as yourself for another person was a great honor for me. What made it better was that I belonged to you."

"You mean that I belong to you." He shook his head, and it was then that she realized they were alone in the big room. Also that the room was finished. "Oh Kip, look at it. It's perfect."

It was, too. The room was large, but it was softened by having three overstuffed couches that made a semi-circle facing the fireplace. There was a fire burning in it now, small yet warming the room to a nice temperature. Over the mantel was the biggest television that she'd ever seen. The coffee table seemed to invite a person to put their feet up on it. It was big enough that snacks and a few bottles of beer could be there too.

There were other touches too. Lamps that were small enough to be unobtrusive, yet bright enough to light the corners of the room. The big windows weren't covered with curtains, letting in the light from out of doors during the daylight hours. Plants of all kinds sat around the room and in corners.

Getting up, she reached for Kip's hand as they looked at the other things in the room. A large braided rug graced the other side of the room where a small sitting area had been made up. A chess set in mid game sat on the top of the little table.

"Are you ready to see the rest of the house?" She nodded at Kip, excited that she'd been able to add some of the things she was seeing in this room. "All right, my lady, let us see what you have dreamed up for our home."

"I don't even mind calling it that." He laughed with her; the feeling of coming home was everywhere. Especially in her heart. "I love it here, and all I've seen is this room. Perhaps you won't like the rest."

"You did it, love. I have no doubt that I will love it as much as I already do you." She didn't comment, but her heart did flutter a bit. "Come on. Let's see the dining room again. And while we're looking, you can tell me the rest of the story about the dock in the middle of the lake."

"Oh, Grandda took me out there, threw me into the water, and made me figure out how to get myself back to him. After I realized that I'd not drown, I learned how to swim." She laughed. "I was lifeguard the next summer at the country club pool. It was fun, and I got to meet a lot of the rich and fabulous in the town we lived in. Not to mention, I made a lot of money that summer, enough to buy my first lottery ticket. With the help of my grandparents anyway. But that was how I started making what would soon be my way out of the house. And onto better things."

"Good for you." She grinned at him just as they entered the dining room. "Now this is a room that I could enjoy with friends and family for sure."

Chapter 3

Luann got on the plane and found her seat. She was pissed off, and she certainly hoped that having bought two seats on this contraption, there would be no one sitting on the other side of her. Sitting in the middle seat, she didn't bother with looking around. The noise was enough to tell her that there were children on this thing. Luann wondered again how come they didn't have other travel arrangements for children instead of a plane where adults wanted some peace and quiet.

"Excuse me, you're in my seat." Luann looked at the man standing above her. "I have that seat. My wife has the one by the window."

"I purchased two seats so that no one would be here to bother me. You must have it wrong. But that doesn't really surprise me. Just go away." He told her again that she was in his seat. "I don't want you to sit here. Find another seat."

"I have these two. Now either move yourself or I'm going to have someone do it for you." She glared at him, something she thought she was quite good at. "Lady, you might think you can make me do what you want with that look, but I just spent the last six years overseas. You're looking at me all pinched up like that doesn't faze me. Now move out of the way."

"I purchased two seats, as I have said to you. You must be reading things wrong. You can read, can't you?" He growled, and she felt the hair on her arms dance. "Look, I'm not moving, so you'll have to figure something else out."

Her heart was pounding, and when a woman dressed in a very tight uniform came to ask what was going on, she stood up to tell her the same thing that she'd told the man. But before she could move, she was pulled out of the seat none too gently, and the man and the woman sat down. Luann curled her hand into a fist, and was ready to hit someone when the uniformed woman spoke.

"Let me see your tickets." Handing over the two tickets that she'd purchased so this sort of thing would not happen, Delilah, the flight attendant, spoke again. "You did purchase two tickets. However, you didn't choose where they were, so they sat them in random places. You are assigned to this seat here on the end. And the other ticket is for the back of the plane, where you are also seated on the end. Now, there will not be any more trouble from you, Miss Mueller, or I'll have you taken from this plane immediately."

Jerking the tickets from her, Luann looked at them. She was right, they weren't together as she had thought. But that didn't mean she was wrong. Luann was going to get her way or else.

"I want my money back for this. I will not be treated like this." Delilah asked her what she thought was going on that was anyone's fault but her own. "I didn't see the option where I could pick my tickets."

"Well, I guess that it sucks to be you." The man laughed and she wanted to hit him. "Please, have a seat or not, Miss Mueller. The plane is ready to go, and you're holding us all up."

Sitting down because she had no choice in the matter, she decided that she was going to talk a mile a minute, just say anything that popped into her head to annoy the couple beside her. Damn it all to hell, this was Louis's fault, and she was going to make sure he understood that she wasn't happy with him for doing this shit to her.

Her plan was foiled as soon as the two of them put on earphones and watched a movie on their phones. Their laughter at it, whatever was going on with the stupid device, was annoying her now. Then the woman got up to go to the bathroom, no less than three times in the short flight. When she wasn't pissing, the man was. Luann felt like a yo-yo, up and down every few minutes.

By the time the plane was landing, Luann was exhausted. Her anger had made her head hurt as well. What really pissed her off more than anything was that she couldn't do a damned thing about it. She was, however, going to make them pay in some way.

Luann stood up as soon as she was allowed to get her carryon. The couple slipped out of the seat just as they'd gotten past her in the first place. Steaming now, she had to wait in line for the people that hadn't bothered with luggage — or had done something else with theirs — until she was able to shove her way into the que. By the time she was out of the long hall leading to the main lobby of the huge airport, the couple was gone.

She hadn't told anyone that she was coming, but when she walked out of the disembarking area, there was a well-dressed gentleman there holding up a sign with her name on it. When she told him who she was, he asked for identification and she pulled out her license. Luann did wonder what he'd have done had she not wanted to show him.

He took her bag from her and led her to the doors. There, sitting in the front of the doors, was the biggest limo that she'd ever seen. The shine on the thing was nearly blinding in the bright sunshine and glaring snow. After the man opened the door for her, she stood there while he put her things in the trunk. Sliding into the limo while he waited, she nearly got out when she saw her sister there.

"What the fuck are you doing, Dalton? Trying to impress me? It won't work. There is nothing you can do that would make me feel anything different for you than hatred." The man that she had just noticed cleared his throat. "What? You think that I should bow down before her because she rented a limo to show off? I won't. She's nothing but a pain in my ass."

"The limo is mine. Dalton and I are getting married soon, and she wanted to make sure that you weren't left in a lurch at the airport." He looked at her like she was nothing but a nasty bug. "You will be civil to her, or I will make your life a living hell. I will too."

"You aren't going to marry her." The man asked her why not. "Just look at her. She's skinny and has no tits. Her face is devoid of anything but those ugly freckles. Her lips are much too large for her face, and she is a pain in the ass."

"My name is Lord Newton, by the way. In reference to your opinion of Lady Dalton, I think her beautiful. More than that, she's fresh and wonderful. As for her being a pain in your ass, I do think that anyone that you didn't like would be labeled as such, so that doesn't mean all that much, now does it? Like the couple on the plane. You should take better care who you are sitting next to next time. The couple were wolves, and could have gladly killed you in a way that would have made everyone that ever met you happy." She said that he was rude. "So are you. Now shut up and enjoy the ride. The hotel where you will be staying is the same one that your brother is in. You'll be happy to know that he's just as pissed off at us as you are, so you two can have fun plotting and planning. However, I would like to forewarn you. Mess with my family, I will kill you."

Nothing more was said by anyone. Luann did wonder about the couple. How did he know that? How on earth did he know they were wolves? She looked over at him and realized that he was one too. Christ, the world was going to hell in a handbasket, and she was going to be the only sane one around.

The hotel that they pulled up in front of was beautiful. It was decorated for the upcoming holiday, and she thought that the trees out front, with their twinkling lights, were pretty. As soon as the door was opened, she could hear a piano over the speakers, softly playing music that sounded lovely. But she said nothing about it, instead huffing her way into the lobby without a backward glance at the two people inside the limo.

Louis was waiting for her as soon as she went to the front desk. A room had been reserved for her. Louis told her that it was next to his and that they could adjoin them. Before she could let go of her anger, he started talking about Dalton and the man, Lord shit face.

"He's a man that I've decided not to mess with." She told him that he was just a man, who thought that he was marrying Dalton. "I believe that he is set on it, Luann, from what I've been told, and this small town seems to know everything, about everyone."

"So? Why do I care what they think they know about our sister?" Louis shrugged as they made their way down the hallway to their rooms. "How did you know that I was coming? Next time you come to get me. Do not send them after me."

"I didn't know you were coming. I saw you coming into

the hotel and waited on you. There is something strange going on around here, Luann. They seem to know things before anyone else does." Throwing her luggage onto the big bed, she asked him what he was talking about. "I don't know. Like they have spies everywhere. And I mean everywhere. I bet if I was to ask, they could tell me what I had for dinner last night, as well as what color my shit was this morning. It's freaky what they know. Like you coming here."

"That's ridiculous. No one has spies everywhere." She did look around the room for cameras and such. "Where do you get your ideas from, Louis? I swear to you, there are times when I think you're off your noodle."

"You just wait and see. In a few hours they're going to know not only what color clothing you brought, but how much too. See. if they don't." Luann had been ready to tell him about the plane incident, but decided that it would just add fuel to his already addled mind. "We're invited to have dinner at the castle tonight. It's all arranged. And if you want to know the truth, Luann, I don't think we were invited so much as we were commanded to be there."

"I'm not going to any castle. What is it, a restaurant or something?" He told her that it was the house of English. "What the fuck is that? I swear, you never explain things so that I can understand you, Louis. What the hell is the house of English?"

"The guy that lives there with his wife, Lady Kendrick, is Fletcher Danburn English, the ninth earl of the English Castle. Danburn, as he goes by, is also a duke of something. Most of the people around here think that he's the king of dragons." She just stared at him, waiting for him to say he was joking. "I'm not, if you're thinking that I'm kidding. He's really all that. Also, there are a group of them here, lords and ladies, dukes and duchesses. A lot of money too, from them to the town."

"You mean they own the town." He told her what he'd heard. "Oh, so they're very generous with their money. I see. They're saps. Why didn't you just say so in the first place? No matter. I'm here to take care of Dalton. And you, for leaving me like you did. Why didn't you tell me that you were coming here?"

"I just wanted to check things out. I went by the grandparents' home. I was going to tell them that I was spending the night so they'd foot the bill for a hotel room. But the house was empty. While I was standing there, I called the realtor to find out what happened." She asked him if they'd finally died. "No, they're living with Dalton and that man that picked you up at the airport. And get this, Luann—she's a lady too. Lord Kipling, the guy she's marrying, is titled, as well as monied."

"So? The newspaper said that she was shot to fuck too, but there she was sitting like she had nothing in the world to worry about." Louis asked her something that she'd been thinking about for a long time. Why did she hate Dalton so much? "I hate her for being born. That should never had happened. I pushed Momma down the stairs so many times, I think toward the end of her pregnancy she was just falling on her own. But to what good? Dalton must have had claws or some shit in there, because she never aborted."

"That doesn't explain why you hate her. I've been giving it a great deal of thought lately, and I cannot for the life of me think why I have hated her so much, other than that you hated her, so I did." She asked him if that wasn't a good enough reason to hate her. "No, I don't think so. She's never done anything to us. Not once has she ever complained about how we treated her. Not that it would have done her much good. Mom and Dad, I think they hated her as well. But damn it, I want to know why we all did."

"Why? Are you thinking that she's been mistreated or something? Is that it? You've had a change of heart, and now you want to get all cozy with her? It's the money, isn't it? You're thinking that now that she has a make-believe title, as well as some ready cash, that you can get some of it? Well, it's not going to happen, Louis. She's just as much a selfish person as she was her entire life. And I, for one, forbid you to do anything but stick with me so that she can be dead. That's all I have ever wanted from her—for her to be six feet under and not a part of my life."

When he left her standing there, she watched him walk through the connecting doors. When the lock sounded on the other side, it was all she could do not to go there and demand that he open the fucking thing right now. Instead, she had to deal with her head aching. Before lying down on the very comfortable bed, Luann took one of her pills to mellow out with. Almost as soon as she was closing her eyes, she thought of how to kill Dalton.

Poison. She'd poison her, and Louis if he kept talking like he was. But Dalton would be out of the way finally.

~*~

Kip had asked her to marry him a total of ten times since she'd turned him down this morning. The ad that had been put in the paper had been for show, to draw out his parents. Apparently, that had worked like a charm. Now Dalton and Kip were at his friend's house, and they were going to be having dinner with them. All of them. Not sure what she was supposed to do with herself, she went to the kitchen where most of the people were gathered anyway. Kip was on the phone with someone.

"Are you settling in all right?" The baby in Kendrick's arms was fussing, and everyone was trying to make it quiet down. "She's not happy that I'm her mom and not her dad."

"I can try something if you don't mind." Kendrick said she would be happy for the help. "Okay, but I did ask."

She let out a shrill whistle that had the glasses shake. But little girl looked at her, eyes full of tears and her lower lip quivering. Taking her when Kendrick said it was all right, Dalton started talking to her.

"Don't you know that you're messing with your mom's psyche? She thinks that you don't like her. That's not so great, is it?" The baby stared at her, but the lower lip was no longer moving. "Look, how about you go back to your mom, smile a big toothless grin at her, and all will be right with your little world? You just can't expect everyone to like you if you're just a whiny ass, now can you?"

Handing the baby back to Kendrick, the baby did just what she'd told it to do. It was probably because Dalton was no longer holding her, but that was all right too. She'd stopped crying, and that was enough for her.

"What did you do?" Dalton assured them that she'd not harmed her. "No, but you did something that I've never been able to do — get her to be happy when I was holding her. What was with that glass shattering sound, too?"

"Sometimes you just have to get their attention. Since I was sure that you'd not appreciate me firing my gun into the air, whistling was the next best thing." Dalton shrugged and the others laughed. "I was a cop for a long time. Then a security guard. Sometimes it just takes someone talking to a person before they realize that what they're doing is shitty, and changing their ways might let them live a little longer."

"It didn't work as often as you would have liked, did it?" She shook her head, and was thankful to Kendrick for changing the subject. "I asked one of the faeries that are keeping track of your family what sort of things they seem to enjoy eating. Then I went ahead and cut that food from our menu tonight."

Dalton laughed. "You are a devil disguised in sheep's clothing, aren't you? But I could have told you. I don't think my sister will come, simply because she was asked to. Louis might. He's been hanging around the town a little more, and might know that Danburn is the king ding dong around here." They all laughed as they put together the biggest salad she'd ever seen. "I guess the faeries are pretty important to everyone. I have one at the house, Button. She's in charge of the house. I'm babbling. I guess you can say that I'm a lot overwhelmed right now."

"We all were at one time. All of us, with the exception of Cassie, were not born dragons. Some of us have since become dragons. Also, most of us have a bit of magic on our own." Dalton asked Quinn, who looked ready to pop with a baby, what the magic might be. "We can touch things and know where it came from, who had it before. My sister, Carmine, has the most power. She uses her mind for all kinds of things. She's learning to control it, but it's been a long road for her. Cassie was born a dragon, as I said, but she can separate herself into nine smaller but no less dangerous dragons. There is some speculation that you have magic now as well. What happened?"

"I was in the hospital, and this creature who turned into a woman told Kip and me how I had saved her. And that she had been protecting me. But now that he was my mate, she seemed to think that I could handle some magic of my own. I don't know what it is. I've not had a lot of—let's call it less overwhelmingness—to see what it is. The faeries looked into my head and decorated and finished Kip's...our house for us. If that isn't enough, I was shot three times just a little while ago, and I don't have a scar or pink mark on me, and I feel better than I have for years. I'm assuming that's what you mean?"

"Yes. I will warn you, Dalton, the being overwhelmed part, it doesn't go away. But you do learn to go with it better." Dalton said she didn't know if she could handle too much more right now.

Danburn's mother walked into the room just then, seemingly hearing the last part of the conversation. "Well, saddle up, young lady, you're in for a treat. Your brother and sister just pulled up." Lady Elissa hugged her as the rest of them left the big room. "You'll be just fine, my dear. Just fine indeed. But if you really want to feel secure, go stand next to Kipling and hold his hand. You'll be surprised at how much that will calm the both of you."

"He asked me to marry him." Lady Elissa asked her when the big day was. "I've not said yes to him. He's so much more than me."

"You mean because he has money?" Dalton told her that she had money of her own. "Then what is it, honey? Is it because he's a dragon? I assure you, Dalton, you couldn't be with a better man than Kipling. Dragon or not, he's the best you could ever want in a spouse."

"Don't you think he's really nice?" Lady Elissa said that he'd better be. "Yes, well, they're all afraid of you, did you know that? But that's not it either. I'm not used to someone being unfailingly nice to me."

"Yes, I can see that. I've heard about your family." She hugged her again. "How about you do as I have asked you to do, and we'll see what sort of trouble these two are going to cause you. By the way, however mean and nasty you think these two are, they're nothing compared to Kipling's parents. Now there is an ungrateful, terrible couple. I have been tempted to pull my dragon and kill them myself at times. Ask young Kipling what happened to him when he stayed here one Thanksgiving."

By the time she told her to ask Kip about that holiday, they were in the front hall. Making her way to Kip, she took his hand into hers. The calmness that she'd been promised was there, and she nearly sighed with it when Kip kissed the back of her hand then nipped gently at her flesh.

"Marry me?" He looked at her with a tight smile. "That way, if you say yes to me, I'll be held back from simply killing your sister. I have never seen a...well, that's not right. My mother is about the same. But she is something, isn't she?"

"Yes." He kissed her hand again, and she wondered if he knew she'd been talking about her sister, not marrying him. It was too late now to correct him, as he was telling the room she had finally said yes. What on earth had she gotten herself into? she wondered.

"Dalton, I'd like to speak to you after dinner, please. Alone." She nodded at Louis, and told him that Kip would be there as well. "Good. That's what I wanted anyway. Thank you."

He walked away and looked at the table that had been set for dinner. She didn't bother counting the place settings — she knew that magic would make sure they had room. Looking up at Kip, she wondered again what she was getting herself into.

"So, Dalton — or should I call you Lady kiss ass Dalton? What is it you have had me dragged here for? Whatever it is, you can know that my answer will be the opposite of whatever it is that you want. I'd also like to know how you're walking around as if nothing happened to you." Dalton started to tell her, but was cut off when Luann started talking again. "I've heard that you're part dragon now. Or was it a bitch wolf? Whatever it is being said about you, I don't believe any of it.

Not a word. Why aren't you dead?"

"I'm smart enough to know that when someone knocks on my door without telling me shit, I shouldn't go to it without being armed. So when he fired, I blew his head off and didn't get to ask him who it was that had sent him. Was it you, Luann? Did you send him to my door to kill me off?" She moved toward the dining room when Kendrick said dinner was ready. "By the way, sister dear, the insurance company is aware that you might have hired someone to kill me off so you could collect on it. He promised me that you'd not be able to put another policy in my name. Not from any group of insurance companies. Shall we eat?"

Everyone was taking a seat when she noticed that Luann was still in the great hallway where she'd left her. Wanting to tell her that no one would serve her out there, Dalton remembered that this wasn't her home. She might have told her if she were in her own home, but not in Kendrick's.

Looking at the other woman now, she smiled when Kendrick told her that she needed to get her attention. Pulling out her gun and laying it on the table, all Kendrick did was put her fingers in her ears. Every other female did the same thing.

Whistling as loudly as she could, everyone stopped talking. Luann, startled by the sound, turned and looked too. Pointing to the only empty seat, Dalton told her that she was holding up dinner. Luann actually stomped her way into the room and sat down. This, Dalton thought, might be more fun that she had anticipated.

"You will not use that vulgar sound again to get my attention. I will not have it, Dalton. I'm your sister, not some cow you're calling to dinner." Kip snickered and Dalton laughed. "You won't think this is so funny if I have to murder her right here."

Everyone stood up at the table. Danburn had a bowl of mashed potatoes in his hand, Rette the platter of steaks. The only people that didn't stand were Luann, herself, and Louis. No one moved. Dalton stood too then, and picked up her gun. Pointing it right at her sister, she made her voice as hard but as calm as she could make it.

"Threaten me again and I won't need them to protect me from you. I will hunt you down like the animal that you are and kill you. I'm not the child you once abused, Luann. I'm a grown person with a family, this family here, beside me. So, if you're not going to listen to what is being said here, then perhaps you should just leave. But if you do, you had better find your ass a seat on the next flight home, because I will come after you. Mark my words, Luann, you do not frighten me any more with your threats and bullshit. Now either shut up or die. Today those are the only two choices that you're going to be given."

"You think you're so big, having that gun in your hand. Well, I'm not leaving until I'm satisfied that I've done what I came here to do." Everyone sat when Dalton did. "I'm not afraid of you either. Come on, Louis, let's get back to the hotel and get this finished."

"I'm not going." Dalton looked at Louis, then at Luann when she asked him what he'd just said to her. "I'm not leaving here. I'm going to talk to them, have a nice dinner, and hope that when they have to kill you for being you, they don't miss and kill me as well. I've only just come to realize what a horrific person you are. I'm not saying that I was much better, but not any more. I'm finished with you as of the moment you walk out that door."

"You're simply sucking up. Come with me, Louis, right now, or so help me, you'll regret it too." Louis stood up and Dalton felt her heart breaking. "Good. I thought you were going to be as stupid as the rest of them here. Come on with me, we'll regroup."

"No, I said I was staying here. I was just going to show you the way out, and make sure that you didn't injure yourself on the way out so you'd have to stay longer. I'm finished, Luann. Goodbye."

When Luann was going out the door, the butler could be heard telling her that he'd called a taxi for her. Whatever Luann might have said to him was cut off when the door slammed shut.

Dalton looked around the table. They were all holding their mirth like it was something precious. Before she could ask them what they'd found so funny, her brother spoke up. He sounded like a small child asking for more soup.

"I hope you don't mind." Danburn assured him that it was fine. "Good. I only just realized that I don't care much for Luann. She's not a nice person."

They all burst out laughing. She joined them. This was the oddest dinner she'd ever been too. But Dalton had a feeling that this wouldn't be the last one she had with these people, nor would it be the funniest. They were a great bunch, and she was glad at that moment that Kip had misunderstood her.

Chapter 4

Dinner was as usual after they laughed at Luann for a while. Even Dalton and Louis did in their own way. No one mentioned Luann again, and for that Kip was grateful. But now he had to be with Dalton while she spoke with her brother. He had a few things to say to him as well if he thought he was going to lay one finger on her, or say a harsh word. She was his, and Kip would protect her with his life, if need be.

Kip wanted to find himself a nice dark corner and take Dalton right then and there. He could have, he supposed, shifted to his dragon and taken her away. But her brother had something on his mind, and Kip wasn't going to take that away from him. It was time they spoke to each other without threats and broken promises. Now was that time. Kip had the rest of their lives to make Dalton his own. Danburn let them use his office when he asked him about it.

"I'm sorry." Dalton asked Louis what he was sorry for. "You know as well as I do that I've been a son of a bitch to you. Both of us have been. And for the life of me, I haven't any idea why we were. So, I asked Luann. She said that she didn't want you born. What kind of answer is that? It's not

49

one—that's what sort of answer it was. I've wasted so many years hating you because she told me to. No, that's not right. I hated you because I was an ignorant fool, and should be shot for just thinking I could be friends with you again."

"You're my brother, Louis." He shook his head and said that he wasn't fit to be anyone's brother. Not yet. "You're going to change yourself? Be something different?"

"I am. A better man. A better person. Anything that I can think to better myself, that's what I'm going to do." He looked at Kip. "You, I would like to call friend as well. But not yet. I have a lot of things to make up for. Not with you, but for myself. I'm ashamed of how I acted, and I'd like to work on that."

"Your sister isn't going to take this easily. She's going to be very pissed at you as well. I wouldn't put it past her to make you her first target in killing one of you off." Louis said that he'd been thinking about that too, and he didn't know what to do about it. "First and foremost, you'll move into our house. If you fuck up while there, I don't have to tell you that one or all of us will take you out. You'll be safer there, safer than you would be in the hotel with your sister."

"I agree. But I can't take up room in your home. I mean, Christ, this is a castle, so I'm thinking that you have a big house as well." Kip told him that they had plenty of room. And that way he could keep an eye on him. "All right. I deserved that. I'll move in. I'll need to wait until I can get in and out of the hotel without seeing Luann, but yes, I'd like that, please. I have a lot of things to let go of. Not anger, but something akin to it. None of it is directed at Dalton either. It's all about me."

"Your things will be at the house when we leave here. Another person that you might want to have as a friend is Danburn. He's a good man, and a better king than we've had in some time." Louis looked at Dalton, then back at him. "Yes,

I'm a dragon. So are all the men you had dinner with tonight."

When he sat down hard on the couch that was in the room, Dalton went to him. She didn't sit with her brother, but she did sit on the floor close to him. She, it seemed, had a great deal to let go of as well.

"What is it you hope to get out of this, Louis? Friendship? Or were you hoping to take back information that Luann could use against us?" Again, Louis said he deserved that, but no, that wasn't his plan. "Then I don't understand. For my entire life the two of you wanted nothing to do with me. Locking me out of my family home. Treating me like I was less to you than the rugs you wiped your feet on. When I left to live with Uncle Eric, you treated him badly as well. I hope you don't expect me to just say to you, 'Okay, we're family again.' I don't know if I can ever be much more to you than a friend."

"Yes, and to be honest with you, Dalton, it would be more than I deserve, or could have hoped for. I never let you into my life. Never did a thing for you other than what Luann told me to do. Not that I couldn't have just backed off and said no, but I didn't. And for that, I have a great deal to make up for." She said that he didn't have to make up for anything, just to be there for her. "I will. That's a promise. I'm not saying that I'm going to be any better at being a friend to you than I was a brother, but I'm going to give it my best."

"I won't take anything you dish out." He asked her if she could give him a hug. "Yes. And I hate to ask this of you, but do you have a knife in your hand?"

"No." Louis looked at Kip. "I'm sorry, sir, but I don't think I can live with you after all. Dalton needs to trust that what I'm saying to her is the truth. I don't blame her for not believing me. Or for that matter, believing in me. I was never anything but a bastard to her. But I think, for all concerned, I should just go home and try long distance for a while."

"Please. I'm sorry. Don't leave. I've had a lot thrown at me this week, and I'm stressed about it. Please, I'd like for you to stay with us. Get to know me and my future husband." Kip smiled at her when she looked at him. "I can't help but think you tricked me into saying yes. But now that you have, I'm glad to be your wife."

"Good. We'll get married in the morning at the courthouse. That way when my parents get here, you'll be the duchess of Winehammer, and be able to order them about like a real lady." Dalton told him that she wasn't ready for that just yet. "Too bad, my love. You are my duchess, and I love you very much."

Dalton left them when Louis said again that he was sorry. She said that she needed to get her brother a room ready, but Kip thought that she just needed a few minutes. Louis looked at him and asked if he could say a couple more things.

"If I fuck up, please tell me. I need to get to know her again, and I won't be able to do that without help." Kip said that he would. "As for Luann. I have a feeling that she's going to try and kill one or both of you. I'm guessing that she'll have about as much chance of that happening as I will being on the top of your best friend list. But if you do have to do something about her, don't make her suffer, please. She might be a bitch and want Dalton dead, but I don't think I could handle making her suffer. Please."

"I don't know what her plans are for either of you. Nor me, for that matter. I will tell you this, however. Her death— because I'm sure you know that will be the only way this ends since she threatened my family—I will try to make it as painless and quick as possible. That's the best I can do." Louis nodded. "But if you come to stay with us for any other reason than to try and make up with your sister, you will suffer. In ways you won't be able to imagine."

Kip was sure that he believed him, and when he left, Louis again said that he was going to be better. Whatever he did, he'd better not fuck up, because Kip wasn't joking around. He would end his life. While he was still in the office, Dalton joined him. When he asked her to sit on his lap, she did so without any questions. Whatever was going on, it was serious enough for her to be thinking about it hard.

"I need to work. I don't suppose you know anyone that would hire a wounded security guard, do you?" He asked her if she'd spoken to Rette. "No, not about needing a job. I didn't think you'd go for it for some reason."

"I'd never stop you from doing what you're good at. Or even anything that you love to do. I work. Not for the money so much as the satisfaction of just having something to do." He looked down at the blouse she had on. "Like right now, I'd like to make it my job of getting you naked and sitting on my cock until you come."

"Wow, that was a nice slide into sex. Do you sit around thinking of these things, or do they just pop into your head?" He grinned at her. "Come on, I'm being serious."

"So was I." He wiggled his brows at her, and she smacked him. "All right. We'll play later. But you want a job, then get yourself one. If it makes you feel any better, all the women work in this family, including Danburn's mom. She works on things like charities that get books and coats for kids. Fills the pantry for the holidays. Elissa is really good at that if you want to help her out."

"I'm not a very good person to ask for things like that. I'm more of a point-my-gun-at-them-and-demand-they-pay-up kind of person." He laughed when Dalton did. "I'd really like to try my hand at being a cop again. I loved it when I did it."

"Why did you stop?" Dalton told him that she'd been

working the streets, and it was too difficult for her to try and save every child on drugs. "Yes, I would see how that would break your heart. I know it would mine as well. There isn't anything like that going on around here. Not that I've ever noticed, anyway. I know that the force here is a good one. No one can be bought. And if anyone questions their loyalty, the officer comes to see Danburn and tells him about it. He keeps the town safe and loyal to us all. That's why we can fly the skies here and not have to worry about anything untoward coming back on us."

"All right, I'll talk to Rette." She stood up, and he was so disappointed that they weren't going to at least neck a little. "If you're serious about us getting married tomorrow, then we'll wait until then to have sex."

"But why?" She laughed, and he tried hard to see the humor in her statement. "I'm still going to marry you, Dalton. I just need you. Very much so."

"One more day won't make that much difference to you." He nodded and she put her hands on her hips, showing off her breasts nicely. "Kipling Newton, one more day will not make your dick explode. You will wait and behave yourself, or I just won't go through with this. Then where will your poor dick be?"

"All right." Even to his ears he sounded like a two year old without a nap. "I guess I can wait one more day. But I want you to know, it's only going to make me crazier for you. All bets are off once you say I do."

She laughed and left him to his pouting. Smiling after she was gone, he called for Button. After telling her what they were doing tomorrow, he told her that he wanted their bedroom to be the most romantic thing she could do for them. Telling Button what he had in mind, the little faerie was making notes. This was going to be epic for Dalton. He only hoped that his poor dick did survive one more night without his mate.

Going out into the living room, he realized that he needed to get his own television hooked up. Mentally making a note to tell Button that, he sat down with the lot of them and watched the game. Thinking about Christmas when an ad came up about it, he realized that the holiday was in ten days and he had a houseful to get gifts for.

At each commercial break he ordered more things. Not only did he not have a tree up yet, but he wasn't even sure that he had any decorations from his childhood. Calling to Button again, he asked her if she could help him with that too.

"We have thought of that too, my lord, and have taken care that everything is decorated within the house. We had a few decorations up, if you remember from today, but we have...I don't remember the exact words that he used, but Mr. Noah said that it looked as if Santa had puked his decorations all over the house. I do hope it was a joke, sir. I thought it looked very good."

"I'm sure that it does. I'll be ordering things for everyone at the house. Tell me, what do the others do for the faeries that work for them?" She told him what she knew. "Good, I can do that. I will do that. Thank you, Button. If you could find me a faerie to work with too, I'm sure I could run them as ragged as I do you."

Laughing, the little person left him. By the time the game was over and they were getting ready to leave, Kip thought he'd gone overboard with gifts. And not by a little, either. He'd be lucky if he got it all in on time, but was happy that he'd had the time to get some of it done.

~*~

Dalton had slept poorly last night. She had only herself to blame in this. She wanted Kip as much as he did her, and like an idiot she'd sent him on his way. Damn it, woman, what is wrong with you? She'd asked herself that about ten times in the last ten minutes. But today she was getting married. Dalton had come to realize that not only did she like Kip, but she loved him as well. It was a gentle sort of falling in love that gave her the belief that it would be the forever kind, too.

The dress she had on was one that she had borrowed from Quinn. Seeing it on the hanger, Dalton had thought for sure that it wasn't her style. But as soon as she put it on, even before she'd had someone zip it up for her, she knew that she'd wear it forever if that was all right with the pretty other woman.

"It feels like silk, but I think it's actually made of cotton. I have another one of the same material that I bought after having this one made for me." Dalton told Quinn that she wanted the name of the shop. "Oh honey, he didn't tell you that you could dress yourself? Kip is a little remiss in that, I think."

"Don't blame him. I've been telling him to give me information on the magic he gave me a little at a time. I can see where that would be at the bottom of the list." Quinn said that she could understand that. "I guess you've had a lot to learn too. Kip told me that your sister is scary powerful too."

"She is. Sometimes I have to remind myself that she can take care of herself. Worrying is what I do best, I think." They both laughed. "I've never met Kip's parents, but I'm told that they're the worst of the bunch of them. Has Kip given you any idea on what they might do when they get here?"

"No. We're sort of taking this one family at a time. My sister wants me dead. I don't even think she knows why she does anymore. My brother, Louis, he's living with us now, but I'm having a hard time simply forgetting about the decades before this. He and my sister didn't have a lot of niceties for

56

me when I was a child."

"I've met your uncle. He's a blast. Eric can tell a joke better than anyone I know, and he can hold onto the punch line too. I usually mess that part up." Dalton told Quinn that she'd never been good at jokes either. But then she'd had to contend with her sister all the time. "I guess all of us women have brought bad family to this one. I'm really glad to know that it's not just me."

"It's also their family. Not one of them, except for Danburn, had a good childhood. You'd not believe what some of them did or wanted from these guys after they were able to rescue the family estate." Dalton asked Kendrick what sort of things. "Well, I'm sure that Kip told you that his parents used the castle that he grew up in as a sort of trash dump. They started in the basement, filling it with things they no longer wanted or were broken. He and Griff had to go in and burn it all out. The grounds too were a mess. They've been planting trees around the place to make it nicer for the faeries and such. Kip is in the process of donating it to the museum so they can use it to show people what it was like to live back then. It'll have to cool down some more. It takes a while. But the cold weather helps a great deal."

Hopefully, Dalton thought, it was going to be modeled after another family and not the one that had lived there.

Dalton was just getting her flowers ready to marry Kip when a woman, a large and overbearing woman, joined them in the room.

"I'm looking for Kipling. Have any of you broads seen him?" No one said a word, but Kendrick did go up to the woman. "Look, lady, I don't know what your beef is right now, but I only want to find my deadbeat brother. Kipling."

"I'm Kendrick, wife to Danburn." The woman dropped so quickly to the floor that it actually shook the building. As she laid there, spread out like she was thinking of being a carpet for the room, Kendrick turned and winked at Dalton. "You will leave here this minute and not return until I summon you. When you return, Bethany Newton, you will be a kinder and gentler person, or so help me, I'll make you regret interrupting my day. Do you understand me?"

The mumbled "Yes, my lady" was just loud enough for them to hear. As the heavy woman, Bethany, slinked her way out of the room and then out of the building, Kendrick came to her. It was Kip's sister; his sister was here, and that could only mean that—

The sting to her face hurt. Looking at Kendrick, she asked her what the hell that was for.

"You were freaking out. Not only that, you were talking so fast that we could barely understand you. They're not here. None of them will show up for another few days. I promise you. Bethany wasn't around when we ordered them away. But she knows better now, and won't come back here until I call for her. All right? Do I need to hit you again?"

"No, once was quite enough." Dalton rubbed the sore place on her cheek. "She's a great deal bigger than I thought she'd be. I mean, I guess I didn't realize that dragons could get that big."

"Fat. It's called getting that fat. Neither did I, just so you know." Kendrick started for the crib where the baby was, but turned back to her. "Look, I need a minute to talk to Danburn. Could you hold Hannah for me for a minute? She seems to like you better than me at times."

"What did I tell you about this?" Dalton held little Hannah to her chest again. "You are giving your mom a complex, young lady. Do you think that is very nice?"

She gurgled at her and smiled. It was the cutest little smile that she'd seen in forever. Talking nonsense to Hannah, she also told her she was about to marry her best friend. When the day was over, she'd be her aunt.

"Or something like that. You'll have a lot of people looking out for you, just so you know. But you come to Aunt Dalton when you need to sneak away and meet up with some friends. No boys, however. Not until you're about three hundred years old, all right? Maybe not even then."

Swaying back and forth, she wondered how she'd be with her own children. They'd not talked about it, Dalton realized. They'd not talked about a great many things, as a matter of fact.

By the time Kendrick came back, Hannah was asleep. Putting her in the cradle with the little faerie watching over her, Pink, the baby's faerie, came to sit on her shoulder. She bowed low and told her that she thought that she was very good with children.

"I'm not, not really. I've not had a lot of experience with them, not this tiny, but I have held them. Mostly because their crack head parents had forgotten about them and nearly starved them to death. Or the baby would be just as high as the parents, so that it would stop crying or some other infraction that the parents had decided they couldn't stand." Pink told her that she was sorry. "Don't be. It was all part of my job. With babies, we saved more than we lost, and I found that to be good enough. It was one of the many reasons that I quit the force when I got shot."

"By a child." She nodded as Pink went back to her charge. "You have had a rough life, have you not? You will be a good mother because of it. Protective, but not overly so. I have seen parents, human parents, hover too much over their young babies. They have a name for it, but I cannot think what it is."

"Smothering. It's what they call it. No, I'd not be that way. Nor will I make sure they win all the time, or get awarded for being on a team. A child must learn, in my opinion, that sometimes you lose, but that doesn't make you a loser. Sometimes you win, but that doesn't make you better than someone else." Pink told her that was a very good way to do it. "Thank you. Button is my house faerie. Do you know if I should have another one? I don't know much about all this as yet."

"I will have Snow come and talk with you about it, my lady. She will know a great deal about everything." Dalton thanked her. "You are most welcome, my lady. I would also like to congratulate you on your wedding. You are a beautiful bride."

The wedding was being held in the courthouse. It was a public place, so there were people going in and out all the time. But most had stopped, knowing most if not all of the wedding party, to see them get married.

Dalton said what she'd been told, a dragon promise to a man that she loved. Kip, in his deep baritone voice, made a promise to her, much like the one he'd given her earlier this week. Before even half an hour had passed on this day, she became Lady Dalton Newton, Duchess of Winehammer Castle.

Lady Dalton. She wouldn't call herself that, she thought, but it was fun to know that she could pull that out when necessary. But for the life of her, she couldn't think of a single moment when she'd have to do that. Not like Kendrick, who used it like a weapon and was damned good at it.

They went back to Danburn's home to have a luncheon. Anyone that wished to come, including the townspeople, were invited as well. That was one of the things that she most liked about these people, especially Danburn—they had no trouble opening their doors to the town. Making the people a part of the family's lives as much as they were a part of the peoples'.

"If you don't come home with me right now, I'm going to toss you to the floor and take you right here in front of all these people." Kip nipped at her ear as he spoke quietly into it. "I'm serious, love. I need my mate more than I have any meal I've ever had."

"You dare compare Lady Dalton Newton, Duchess of Winehammer Castle, to a hamburger? For shame, Lord Newton." She looked around and smiled up at him. "I have it on good authority that there is a wonderfully quiet room all set up for us in the pool house not far from here."

She was standing in the little house in seconds. And she was naked. Giggling as Kip rushed to take his own clothing off, she nearly fell over when he was finally as naked as she was.

"Oh my, Kip."

Chapter 5

Kip had forgotten that she'd not seen his body. When she touched the scar that ran down his chest, he let her, cooling his body off so that she could see what she'd gotten in a husband. When she started asking him about them, he didn't want to tell her, but his dragon spoke to him for the first time in his life.

She will need to know all, my lord. For without knowledge, she will be hurt when they come. He said that they had time for that. *Nay. Your sister showed herself today. She is most fat, but Bethany could have hurt Lady Dalton had Lady Kendrick not stepped in.*

Dalton's fingers ran the length of the scar, asking him again what had happened to him. Kip thought about lying to her, telling her it was a battle scar, but decided that his dragon was correct, she'd need to know.

"When I was about ten, my brother Kenneth decided that he wanted to see what was beneath the skin of someone. Since he'd been beating on me for years, he figured that I would make a good candidate for his experiment." She kissed the scar at both ends. "He tied me to the wall, calling to the rest of my family to come and see what I was made of. The knife that

63

he had was nothing more than a rusty blade that he'd found. I believe he thought it was iron. Thankfully it wasn't. Kenneth only managed to get the single cut along my chest before I was able to free myself and attack. It was the greatest feeling I've ever had. For all of about five seconds, until the rest of them pounced on me too."

"I've yet to meet them, and I hate them badly enough to kill them all." He said that it was worse than that. "This one here, it looks like a burn. Did he try to burn you at some point as well? Did he want to see how fast you'd roast?"

"Something like that. He rammed a white hot poker from the fireplace into me." He turned around, holding her body to his. "Every scar that I have on me is from one or all of them. Most of them will disappear when I can make a stand against my father. Kenneth had been deemed unfit to be the king of the castle; my father is barely holding on to his title. The castle, as I told you, was filled with ruin. My mother, the very opposite of Elissa, never hugged, told me that she loved me, or did one thing motherly to me. Fletcher, Danburn's father, was more of a dad to me than my own was. And Elissa a mother that I didn't have."

"I'm sorry. I was speaking with Pink today, and she said that I'd make a good mother. I realized that we'd never talked about having children." He nodded and asked her if she wanted any. "I do. I really do. I know that we're going to be around for a very long time, but to be honest with you, Kip, I would love to have a child with you as soon as we can."

"I would love that as well. And if you'd not mind, adopting children would be wonderful as well. Some that have had an abused life. Children that need someone to tell them that they're special, that they're loved. I want to help as many children as we can, whether we adopt them or not. All right?"

"Yes. That would be wonderful." Kissing her again, Kip looked down at her. Smiling up at him, she felt like she'd finally come home, that someone loved her. "Make me yours, Kip. You and your dragon's mate for all time."

The kiss was gentle. It wasn't as consuming as the one that he'd given her last night, but she knew that he wanted her. His cock was there at her pussy, and she could feel herself getting wetter and wetter with each touch of his fingers to her body.

"I need to taste you." She shook her head. "You have no idea how badly my dragon wants me to taste you so that he can as well."

"I want to taste you first. I need to know how you taste. Just how hot your juices will be when they slide down the back of my throat." Dalton wrapped her hand around his thickness, moaning when he did. "When I'm finished with you, if I ever am, you can have your fill of me."

She might have waited for him to say something, but she was eager to have him, to know the things that she'd said. Taking him into her mouth, Dalton felt her body come, a hard blast to her body that made her only want more of him. When she cupped his balls into her palms, Kip wrapped his hand into her hair and held her still.

Dalton fondled his balls until they were tight against his body. Each time she swallowed around him, tasting the juices that were flooding her mouth, he would fuck her mouth harder. It was a give and take thing they were doing. She was giving him pleasure, and in turn he was filling her with his seed.

When she swallowed the next time, just as he was pushing forward, his head, hard and full, passed beyond her tight throat and she screamed around his cock when he cried out. Each time he fucked her now, it was like he was touching the back of her head, down her back and to her feet.

Sliding her fingers into her wetness, she touched her clit, crying out against the convulsion her body had as her own pleasure rippled around her. Then he filled her body with his release.

It was too much for her, and she felt long streams of it touching her breasts as it slipped past her lips. When Kip pulled back, Dalton licked his cock, taking in as much as she could of him. Before she could do much more than taste him again, she was up off the floor and slammed against the wall. Kip took her then, pounding her hard.

"Bite me, Dalton. Take me into your body, blood and soul." She didn't know if she could do that, bite someone hard enough to draw blood. Shaking her head, Dalton wasn't ready for that, she thought.

When he bared his neck for her, her mouth watered. It was like he was offering her a large platter of food, her favorites. Licking her tongue along the pounding pulse she could see there, she opened her mouth wide and felt something moving over her teeth. Biting Kip there as hard as she could, the taste of his blood filled her mouth, and Dalton came hard enough that she blinked out for several seconds.

Waking, she was on the floor. Kip was still deep inside of her, his cock moving slowly in and out of her. Looking down at her as she wrapped her fingers around his shoulders, he smiled at her as he took her just a little harder, his cock filling her to the root of him. Her legs wrapped around his, pushing her body up to each of his downward strokes.

"You're very sexy looking all tousled like you are." She giggled, then asked him about the bed that was right over there. "Nah. What would we have been able to tell Danburn if we broke it? This is much safer for us. I know that there is a lower floor in this place, and we might just end up there anyway."

He took her breast into his mouth then, taking her body to new heights. Her mind was so overwhelmed by every emotion and feeling. Telling him that she wanted to come, needed to, he leaned into her face, kissing her mouth hungrily until she thought that he was going to have her for a meal.

"Please, I want to come. I need to."

He took her hard, her body no longer her own as he touched her skin, the heat of it feeling as if they were becoming one. Just as she thought that she was never going to fall over the summit of pleasure, Kip lifted her bottom up and took her deeper than before.

Her scream was primal, a beast roaring up from inside her to wrap around her heart and head. When she came a second time, Kip cried out as well, his own beast showing his head to her as his heated cum filled not just her body, but everything, every cell of her. Then she did blink out. Or more likely she had died and had gone to pleasure heaven.

Dalton woke warm. Trying to get away from the heat, she was pulled back into his arms. Kip. She was married to the man lying next to her. Instead of going back to sleep as she should have done, as it was dark out still, she looked at the man she had pledged her life to. When he opened his eyes and smiled at her, she decided to get some information before his family and hers ruined their day.

"The scars. You know how each of them were put there, don't you? You remember them like they were only put there yesterday." He nodded and frowned at her. "I have a lot of them as well. Some from my family, some from my job. I have an idea of how we can try to rid ourselves of not only the scars, but the memories of them as well."

"I don't know if I can do that, love. Some of them are very deep. Not just on my body, but my heart as well." Dalton told him that she wanted to fill his heart. When he rolled to his back and pulled her over him, Kip kissed her. "All right. I'll do whatever it takes so that you are the only thing in my heart. What's the idea?"

"We write them all down on sheets of paper. Just how they were put there. Not feelings behind them, just how." Kip nodded and told her to go on. "We put them in a jar that each of us own. And when something good happens, something that makes us feel good about ourselves, we pull one of them out and destroy it with your dragon."

"How do you know that will work? As I said, mine are deep." She nodded and showed him the one over her heart. The surgery scar that had removed the bullet that had touched her heart. "All right. I'm going to give this my best. We should limit it to just family things then. I have battle scars that I'm proud of. Things that I did to save a castle, save a family. All right?"

"Yes, I can get on board with that." Kip kissed her again. "Should I wonder how we got here, to our house? And wonder how much damage we did to Danburn's pool house?"

"The pool house is fine. I repaired anything we broke." She laughed with him. "As for coming here, it's magic that I have. I can move us through space quickly. I have to tell you, love, that I barely had enough energy to bring us here. You nearly killed me."

They were both in such a wonderful mood that she didn't mention that his sister was at the wedding yesterday. They took a long hot shower together, washing each other and making love again. She was sore, Dalton told him, but he was gentle with her this time.

Breakfast was on the table when they came down the stairs. Dalton met their new cook, Allison, and found out that she was a foundling. After that was explained to her, a newborn faerie that had been left behind, she was glad for the extra protection in the house. There were others there too, but Button was right by her side the entire time.

After they ate, the two of them walked around the land that they owned. Talking about nothing really, just about fun things, she was startled when Kip suddenly stopped talking in mid-sentence and looked at her.

Your brother went to talk to your sister last night. She nodded, knowing that to have trusted him was a mistake. *She murdered him. I'm so sorry, love. Apparently Louis tried to talk her into giving up on her plan to kill you, and she shot him five times in the chest. He never had a chance to get away.*

Where is she now? Her mind was still trying to work out that Louis was dead and that he'd been there for her when she looked at Kip because he didn't answer her. *Where is she, Kip?*

Behind you. She didn't move when he grabbed her arms. *Don't move. She can't see you or me right now. I'm holding us in darkness until the rest of them get here. The police are on their way as well.*

She's here to kill me. Just like she did Louis. He nodded. *I don't understand this, Kip. I never did a thing to either of them. Just when I was getting ready to —* You know what? Fuck this waiting shit. I can handle her.

Before he could stop her, even if he was going to, she turned around and saw that not only was Luann close enough to nearly touch her, but she had her gun in her hand as well. Dalton took a step forward and slapped the gun out of her hand.

"What the fuck are you doing here? Why? I want an answer to that before I do what I should have done years ago." She could see the insanity then. Luann was wearing it like an armor around herself. It was sad and scary at the same time. Dalton asked her again what the hell she was doing.

"My little sister is finally going to meet her end. Yes, I killed Louis. He was turning into a pussy. I can't have that around me. You have to die." When she jumped for the gun, Dalton punched her sister in the face.

~*~

Kip tried very hard not to laugh. It was that or he was going to have to shift and take out the entire group of people that were there with them. No one was hurt, thankfully, but he was sure that no one was going to forget this for as long as they lived. He knew that he certainly wouldn't.

"I just need five more minutes with her." Danburn was holding Dalton back as Kip sat on the ground, where he thought he might be safer. "You let me go and I'll give you all my money, Danburn. Just let me hit her once more before they take her away."

"You're a vicious little thing, aren't you? Just hold your horses a little while longer. The police are taking care of her now." Dalton looked at him, her lower lip swollen but not bleeding. Each time he looked at her, he had to laugh again. Danburn just glared at him. "Kip, instead of laughing your fool ass off, get up and take care that she doesn't turn over the cruiser and get to her sister again. Damn it, but she's going to do it, I just know it."

Laughing, he finally got up. Danburn shoved Dalton at him and he nearly missed the handoff. She was off again, going after the car that Luann was in the back of. He would never piss her off again just to see her get all huffy, he decided. Dalton was out for blood, and he was having a hard time holding her back.

The cruiser was pulling away from where they all were when Dalton finally relaxed. She was pissed; it was like she was wearing it, her skin was so hot with it. When she told him she was fine, for about the tenth time, he finally believed her.

Licking her lower lip to heal it, he looked at Danburn when he asked what had gotten into Dalton.

"Her sister just showed up right after you told me about Louis. I had us both covered so that she'd not see us, but Dalton felt that she had to deal with this once and for all. I think that she needed this. Right now she looks beaten, but I have to tell you, Danburn, she was as high strung as I'd ever seen any of us. After slapping the gun away from her, Luann went for it." He laughed again and stopped when Elissa cleared her throat. "Sorry. But Dalton just drew back her fist and hit her sister square in the nose. I mean, it was a prize winning punch too."

"Kipling, you do go on, don't you?" He looked at Elissa, then back at Dalton, who was just standing there. "Dalton, you didn't hit your sister, did you? Honestly?"

"I did. And I would have done a lot more had he not pulled me off her. She killed my brother. Hitting her was better than she deserved." Dalton looked at Kip. "You were right to pull me off of her. Killing her like I really wanted to do wouldn't have solved anything. Nor would it have settled anything in my heart."

"Luann confessed to killing their parents." Elissa hugged Dalton while she cried. Kip finished the story while she was getting comfort only a mom with a big heart could have given her. Kip knew that feeling first hand. "After knocking her around a couple of times, Dalton asked why she'd killed Louis. She told her that it was because he'd been tainted by Dalton. She also tried to tell Dalton that it was all her fault, but Dalton wasn't taking it. Instead, the two of them fought for a few minutes more before not only did she confess to killing their parents, but that it had been a good thing that she'd done too."

"Why?" Kip looked at Dalton. It should be her telling

71

what she'd gotten from her sister. Everyone looked at her when she let go of Elissa. Rette asked again why Luann had done it.

"Luann told me that they'd changed in their golden years. That they'd been sorry for all that they'd done. Even going so far as going to church again on Sundays so that they could feel much better about themselves before they came to see me." Kip held her when Dalton leaned against his chest. "It made her mad that they'd had such a change of heart about me, and she just couldn't have that, she told me. Not with her and Louis planning to murder me in the coming months. I guess it was about the time that Louis figured out that Luann had killed them that he started thinking that there was something wrong with Luann. I could see it as well, the madness in her eyes."

"She needs help." Dalton nodded at Em when she spoke. "It's more than that, isn't it? I mean, she told you more than you thought about her killings."

"Yes. Luann has been murdering people for some time now." Dalton looked at Kip. "I don't know why I didn't put it together before, but she also killed my Aunt Sue, Eric's wife, the man who worked in the meat department, and a few others. I didn't have to have her tell me that. When I held her, her blood touched me and it was like I had an open pathway to her mind. I could see them all. I even know where the bodies are."

"I can help you with that." Dalton nodded at Rette and thanked him for it. "I wanted to talk to you anyway, Dalton. I'd like for you to help me out by taking over the police department when you're up to it. The chief that we had there until last week has retired. This might be just the thing you need to see other things taken care of too."

"I was coming to talk to you too. I don't know about chief,

but I would like to work for the police department. Thanks." Danburn asked if there was anything else they needed to take care of right now. "I have to go down and press charges. Though I think they got her for a lot of other things too. I also want to go and give them the names of the people that she's murdered. I swear to you, I never thought that she had done this before. I did think she murdered our parents, but it was just something I thought about, never really questioned before."

"Sometimes it's just hard to believe that anyone you know is capable of such things." Kip knew that Griff's words were truer than Kip could explain to him. His family was just as bad, just as murderous. "Why don't we get home, have a nice meal, and then put this to bed for a while? I, for one, have a lot of gifts to wrap yet."

"Holy shit. I forgot I have stuff coming in." Everyone laughed when Kip suddenly yelled. "I forgot about Christmas until we were watching the game. Up until then I'd not done a single thing. I still have to go shopping."

Dana laughed. "It can wait until tomorrow. In fact, Em was just saying that she wanted to get you guys gathered up to go shopping for the day. What do you say we make some reservations somewhere, and spend the next two days doing just that? Shopping." Everyone nodded, and Kip was getting into the spirit right along with them. "All right. Tomorrow after breakfast, we all gather up at the airport at about eight and leave from there. I'll take care of the reservations as well as the flight plan."

It was set. Tomorrow they'd go shopping and forget about everything else for a few days. They'd be back just in time to deal with his family. Smiling, he thought he'd just sic Dalton on them and that would be the end of it. The only one he didn't have to worry about was Kenneth. He was in prison, and would be there for a few more decades. Shaking his head, he knew that he'd not be so lucky. It would be his luck that—

"My lord, do you have a moment?" He walked away from the rest of the group holding Dalton's hand. Whatever was going on that would bring Button here, he knew that it couldn't be good. "I was just speaking with Mother Earth. She said that there is some movement that you must be made aware of."

"My brother has escaped, hasn't he?" Button nodded. "I knew it. I just knew it. And how did he escape, do you know that as well?"

"Your parents have decided that they'd like for him and your sister to live in the castle again with them. They are on their way there now." Dalton asked how long they had. "With the delays that we have given them, the other faeries, they will be here sometime after the holiday. We will continue to put things in their way for longer if we can. They are not happy with the way things are going, my lord. They are...what did Snow say? Ah, they are hopping mad."

"What are you doing to delay them, Button? As much as I'd like for them not to come here, I don't want any of the faeries to be harmed in any way. Make sure that whatever you're doing also won't get you into trouble, all right?" Button nodded at Dalton. "No, tell me that you're not going to get hurt by what you're doing, and no one is going to be going to jail for it."

"We are being very careful, my lady. They are only being delayed by making sure that there is no place to rest their heads at night. Food too is not very plentiful, as we are forewarning the animals to steer clear of them. Dragons need to consume large amounts of food to fly." Dalton said that was all right then. "Thank you for being concerned for our welfare. It shows me yet again what a great mother you will be to your own dragons."

They were in the house when Dalton turned to him. He could see the panicked look on her face, and wondered what had happened now. But when she grabbed his shirt and pulled him in for a kiss, he hugged her. Then she grabbed his hair.

"*Ouch*. What was that for?" She yanked harder on his head. "Really, honey, tell me what I did wrong so that I can fix it for you."

"I want you to tell me whatever it is that I need to know. I'm sick of getting this stuff in bits and pieces. Also, if you think I'm going to have a baby dragon come out of my body, I will take your dick off you and hang it from the highest trees, you hear me?" He said that he heard her loud and clear. "Will I have a baby dragon?"

"Yes, but not like you think. Because you're not a dragon, you will have a baby first, and then it will later turn into a dragon. If you were the dragon in this relationship, you'd have an egg that would be born a dragon. Can you let go of my hair?" She did. He finished telling her the rest while rubbing his head. "The egg is small at first, no bigger than a normal sized baby. But as the child grows then so does the shell around him. But you don't have to worry about that. I cannot convert you to a dragon, sadly."

"Okay. But please tell me things like that so I'm not in the dark. I just want to make sure that I'm not having a kid and it turns out to be a fucking dragon." Kip smiled at her. "You are not as adorable as you might think you are when you smile like that."

"Yes, I am, and you know it." Kip hugged her again. "We'll go away with the family, have some nice dinners out, and forget about everything but each other. All right? Do you have a list made up?"

"I'm going to work on one after we eat. You can help me with that." He said it would be his pleasure. "This tree is beautiful I've not had a tree since...well, since forever, I think. The last one I remember was at Uncle Eric's house when his wife was alive."

"Are you going to tell him what you've found out?" She said it would be better coming from her than in the courtroom. "More than likely yes. I'll go with you. That way if he wants to be upset and all manly like, I can be there for him."

"Yes, because you're all manly." He smacked her butt as they made their way to the dining room. A menu from the local restaurants was being passed around and they had to choose. Kip was ready for something to fill his belly. Also something different to fill his mind. He could not wait for this all to be over with.

"Where is your uncle anyway?" Everyone dropped their heads. He looked around and decided that this was going to be bad news too. Dalton seemed as confused as he was. "Danburn, what's going on?"

"We saw them coming out of the pizza shop the other day." Dalton asked him who he'd seen. "Your uncle and Marissa, Griff's mom. They looked like they might have been having a good time, too. It's about time that she found herself some happiness. Even if he's not her mate, I think both deserve to have some good in their lives."

"I agree." Kip looked over at Dalton when she said nothing. "One of the things that Luann confessed to was killing Sue, Eric's wife. I don't know how long it's been, but to see either of them happy is all right with me."

He and Danburn went to pick up the food. There was going to be a great deal of it, so they took a car instead of the truck this time. He thought the food would get cold sitting in the bed of his truck, as it was only a two door. Kip had a feeling that Danburn had something on his mind, and they were barely out of the driveway when he finally spoke.

"They'll be killed, you know." Kip nodded and said that he'd have no problem with that. "Yes, I didn't think you would. But if things progress as they did before, we'll have four dragons to find human's for."

He nearly drove off the road. Turning to look at Danburn, he spoke when he thought he could. "You trying to ask me something about these dragons you're going to have to find humans for? Or are you just trying to have me drive us off the road and into a ditch so we don't eat tonight?"

"Just the first one. You seem to have a handle on not driving us into a ditch." Kip was going to murder his best friend. "I was thinking that you'd take one of them for Dalton. Then if they really are an item, I can give one to Eric. To be honest with you, Kip, I really like the man. Even if they only hang out together, I'd like to have him around for a while."

"Me too. He's been in and out of the house the last few days. I think it would be wonderful to have him around. What about her grandparents? Should we ask them?" Danburn told him that they'd already expressed a desire not to be made immortal. "I can see that. They're in their late seventies now, aren't they? Yes, I can see that."

"Good. Then you talk to Dalton about it, and I'll talk to Mother Earth. Maybe she knows someone that might benefit from having a dragon in their corner."

Two dragons. He didn't mention the wives that didn't have dragons. They were powerful enough in their own right, and they didn't know what could happen if a dragon was in the mixture.

"Kip, you missed the restaurant."

Chapter 6

Kenneth was sick of being cooped up in the house. He knew why the rest of them could go out and not him, but it didn't make it any less annoying that he couldn't go with them. They didn't even bother bringing him back anything.

"Stop acting like a child. We got you out of jail, didn't we?" There were days when he disliked his father. More and more of late he wanted to kill him. If not for his mom, he might well have done it. "Jehoshaphat, boy. You'd think that the world only moved because you were in it. Well, it doesn't. Nor does the sun shine right out of your ass either. Just in the event you was thinking on that."

"I could really hate you right now." Father just laughed, as he always did when he was pissed off. "The only reason that I was in prison was because you and Bethany left me behind with the goods when we was robbing the bank. The least either of you could have done was to let me know that you were leaving so that I could as well. But no, you had to just take off, leaving me to take the hit. Did I turn you in? No, I didn't. I suffered through being a fucking human until I could figure out a way to leave without killing the entire population of the prison."

His father had had no such qualms about it. Luckily for everyone, they were in the yard when his father had decided to heat the bricks up to get him out. Only seven had been on his side of the building when he'd done it, or it might have been so much worse. Not that he thought anyone would care about the dead inmates. Neither did he, to a point. It was just the fact that his father never thought of these things when he had an idea. The concept of the idea was fine. The consequences not so much.

Now that he was out, all his father could talk about was going back to the castle and living. Yes, because that wouldn't be the first place that the council would look for them. Besides, when they'd left, it had been a shit hole of a place anyway. Why anyone would want to go back there was beyond him.

"It's cleaned up." Kenneth looked at his mom when she spoke quietly. "Kip, he went in and cleaned it all up for us. I'm sure that he didn't do it for us, but it's nice and cleaned up right now. Your dad, he sent Bethany to spy on Kip, and she said that not only was it cleaned out, but that it was too warm for anyone that wasn't a dragon to go into. I kind of like that we get to start new, don't you? I mean, think of all the things we can buy to put in it."

"What do you think we're going to use for money? Last time I looked, none of us had any power to make enough for food." He looked down at the leftovers that he'd had for his own dinner. "How are you paying for all this? I'm sure that the council hasn't found it in their hearts to let us have our tears back."

"No, they've not done that yet. But we had a little left from the robbery that we've been using. Not much more of it left, though. I don't know what your father will do to fix that situation, but I know he will." Kenneth thought that was why he'd been broken out. He was going to have to go with his father to get them more money. He asked his mom if she knew any plans. "No. He did mention Kip and getting him to cooperate. But I really don't think that is going to happen, do you?"

"No. Not unless he's forced to do it." He knew, even if they didn't, that Kip had taken a mate. The earth had rattled so badly that he'd fallen out of the bed he'd been in. "What do you know of his mate? He took one, you know."

"Oh. I never thought of that. Yes, I guess that might have been what shook the house so badly. But who would he get? I mean, he doesn't have a thing. The castle belongs to your father. Then it goes to you after your father is ready to give it up. But I'd not count on that for some time yet, Kenneth." He wasn't counting on it at all. "We'll just have to reason with him. Or barring that, take his mate, whoever it might be, and get what we need. He should be nicer to us, you know. He's still alive, isn't he? Kip was never like you two. You and Bethany were our pride and joy, you know."

He didn't bother answering her. They all felt like Kip was odd man out. Or in this case, odd dragon out. He was always going to Fletcher too. The bigger dragon would take Kip to the council, then he'd clean him up, feed him well before Mom or Father would go and get him, and it would start all over. Even hiring someone to kill off his younger brother had never worked. Kip seemed to have had this magic over him that kept him from being killed. Kenneth decided to have a look into that when he saw his brother again.

Going to the room he was using, he sat on the bed. The house they were living in wasn't large, but the beds sure were nicer than he'd been used to. Four years in prison would make any bed feel better, he supposed. The food certainly wasn't that much different, he thought.

Hey, come down here. I have to talk to you. Kenneth told his dad that he was done talking to him. *You want me to call the cops back up on you, boy? I will. If you're not going to help out, then you might as well be back in the jail house. You're not doing me a bit of good out here.*

Stomping his way back down the stairs, he wondered what would happen if he were to shift and burn the house down around his parents. Nothing, his dragon told him. They were dragons too. Like he needed advice from him on how to treat his father.

"We have to go into town. We're going to need us some money soon, and I can't do it on my own." Kenneth didn't say anything to him, but waited. He'd bet anything that his dad thought that robbing anything, like another bank, was going to be a piece of cake. "I'll go in the bank first, and then— What are you shaking your head no for? It's worked before."

"For you it worked out nicely. For me, I had to spend four years of my life behind walls while you enjoyed the money that you took out and left me behind. No, you want to rob a bank, then I'm going to go in and stake things out. You come in and rob the place." Father drew back his fist as if he was going to hit him. "Do it. Come on, hit me if you think you can live through me hitting you back. Don't forget, I'm younger and stronger than you are."

"I fucking hate you." Kenneth didn't let him see how it had hurt him. He wasn't even sure why it had hurt so badly. He didn't have all that much love for him either. Going back up to his room, he laid on the bed thinking about his lot in life.

He thought about Kip. How if he did have a mate, how happy he'd be about now. The man had more luck than anyone he'd ever met. Kenneth even thought that if the house was cleaned up as Mom said, they'd not be able to enter. Kip was lucky, but he was also the smartest man or dragon that he knew.

There was going to be something surrounding the castle that would not only prevent them from entering, but would also alert the council. He wasn't going to lose any more of what little powers he had left. It was bad enough that they'd lost their money makers. All because Kip had found out about their plan to have him killed. Kenneth rolled to his side and thought about that for a moment. Why were they trying to kill him?

As far back as he could remember, Kip had done nothing to any of them. Yes, he'd turned them in when they'd hurt him. But what did they expect to happen? That he'd just let them turn him into a dead dragon? He would have done the same thing, Kenneth thought.

Bethany was the worst about hating Kip. He thought it was because she'd been the baby of the family, and Kip had taken her place when he was born. Like that had made a difference in how she'd been treated. She still got her way in everything. It wasn't as if any of them had ever wanted Kip around. But why?

He had no answer to that. Only that his parents and he and Bethany had fucked up, over and over, and Kip hadn't. Was it because they thought he'd been too good for them? Nah, no one cared if he was the good guy or not. It had only made him a bigger target. Because he'd had more friends than them? No, that couldn't be it. None of them had liked people all that much, or dragons either for that matter. Everyone, he remembered thinking when he'd been younger, everyone had always been content with their lot in life. Being a dragon and having what they wanted. But his family had always been greedy for more.

Thinking about Kip, he decided to reach out to him, to see if he could have a conversation with him. Kenneth also thought about his mate, who she might be, what sort of person she was.

She'd be like him, he thought. Nice to the point of annoying. Kenneth didn't like that answer either. It was mean. While he thought of himself as bad assed, he didn't like the way it made him feel when he'd thought that about his brother's mate. Kenneth wondered now if he had ever had one out there, waiting on him to find her. Or, like most of the things in his life, had he fucked that up as well? He did something that he thought he might regret, and did reach for his brother.

Yes? Again, it hurt Kenneth to hear the suspicion in his brother's voice. *What is it you want, Kenneth? I'm not going to give any of you any money. I don't believe that you can beat me up again – I'm stronger now. If you harm anyone that I now consider family, there will never be a place you can go that I won't hunt you down like the animal that you have become.*

I deserve that. He didn't know what else to say. He wasn't used to this Kip. He sounded stronger, his anger almost something that he could touch, even through their link. *I guess you have a mate now. Is she pretty?*

Yes, beautiful. She loves me too. Of course she would. Kip was a nice guy. *What is it you want, Kenneth? As I said, I have nothing to give to any of you if that's why you wanted to speak to me.*

I don't know that I wanted anything. I've been thinking, and I wondered about why I had hated you so much. Maybe you knew. He could almost feel his brother's shock. *I've been broken out of prison. I wanted to tell you, too, that Mom and Dad plan to take the castle back.*

What about you? You think to take it back with them? Kenneth said that he was content where he was. *I see. Do you really expect me to think you've had a change of heart about me? As for*

84

your question, no, I have no idea why you all hated me so much. Every time you met up with me, there was a different reason for why you wanted me dead. Anywhere from just being born, though I doubt any of you realized that it wasn't my doing to be born, to some slight that you felt was my fault when it rested entirely on your shoulders.

He was right, but that didn't really give him much of an answer. Was he having a change of heart? Doubtful. Kenneth told himself that he was bored, that was why he'd contacted his brother. But that wasn't entirely true either.

To be honest, Kip, I'm not sure why I contacted you. I've been doing a lot of thinking since I was in prison. It wasn't that bad, being there. Not really. I had a roof over my head that I didn't have to steal from someone else. Three meals a day that were good. He was getting off track and knew it. *I was just wondering why anyone would hate you. Especially family. I mean, sure you were different than us. But that wasn't a bad thing. Bethany really hates you. Again, I have no idea why, but she does. I thought it was because you were the youngest and she wasn't anymore. But that didn't change her getting everything she wanted. I did too. I know that.*

Why don't you come to the point, Kenneth? It wasn't anger he heard in his voice this time, but something like curiosity. *I don't know what you want from me. I'm not even sure that I like you anymore either. I know that it's harsh, just to say it like that, but after the way the three of you treated me, I don't know how you can expect anything more from me.*

No, I don't. And I'm sorry to hear that. But not surprised by it. He thought of what he really wanted. *I've just decided something. I'm going to leave here. Leave Mom and Father and just go away. I'll report to the council. That's what I'll do. I'll go to them and let them do what they will with me.*

Why? He told Kip that he wanted to just be alone. *You*

enjoyed that? Being all by yourself? You do know that they're either going to end your life or they're going to put you in prison, one that you'll never be able to break out of.

Yes, I'm sure that it'll be the first one. But as of right now, talking to you, I know that it's no less than I deserve. His brother was quiet for a few seconds, and it gave Kenneth time to think. He was going to do it. For the first time in his life, he really felt as if he was on the right path. *No matter what they decide to do, Kip, I'm feeling pretty good about it. Like even if I were to have to die, I know that this is what I was meant to do.*

I have done something for you. It's going to cost me something from Danburn. But I'm willing pay the fines for it. I have given you freedom. Kenneth sat up on the bed, his heart pounding hard. He knew what the words meant, but he just didn't want to believe that his brother would do such a thing for him. *You must leave now, Kenneth. If you leave now and have no contact with anyone in the family, including me, you will forever be free of them. But the first contact that you have with them —*

I won't. Not ever again. He got up, looked around the room, and decided that there was nothing there that he needed. Taking the pillow and a blanket, he asked him what this would cost him. *I don't want you to have the same fate as I have, Kip. That wouldn't be something that I wanted.*

You did the right thing just now. Thought of someone else other than yourself. Go to the bank closest to where you are. National Bank on Tenth. Go there and just tell the teller your name. She'll give you an envelope. Get it and go. All right? Go and never return. He promised him again that he wouldn't. This was more than he could ever have hoped for. *I don't like you, Kenneth, but you are my brother, and I do love you.*

Kenneth started sobbing. He just couldn't form any words that would come through his strangling emotions. Nodding, he left the house without seeing his mom and father. Once he was out in the yard, he walked, not taking the car that had been in the garage when his family stole the house they were living in. Once out the door, he felt free, like he was atop the world. Kenneth would do just as he said he would, would make good on the promise that he'd made to Kip and do better. He was going to be a better man.

The bank teller handed him the envelope, which was thick. Taking it to the bus station, he sat down on the bench there and opened it. Inside was a great deal of money. Taking out what he thought he would need, two hundred dollars, he put the rest in the pillow that he had.

He would need traveling things. Going to the store that was closest to him, he got himself a large piece of luggage, all the toiletries that he thought that he'd need, and some snacks to eat. Clothing too was stuffed into the cart. When he was at the register, he started loading things onto the belt, and realized as things were being rung up that he might have gotten too much.

"Can you tell me your name, please?" He told the cashier. "Okay, your brother said to tell you that you have done well again and that he has paid for this. But he said to remind you that you will need a few bottles of water for the trip." He got them out of the little fridge next to him and she rang them up. "Kip said to tell you also that you won't get any more free gifts from him. But he wanted you to have a good start on the rest of your life."

The total came to just under six hundred dollars. Stuffing everything he could into the luggage, which turned out to be a four piece set, he went back to the bus station. There he got the first ticket out for the destination the furthest away. Kenneth was well on his way to being a new man. And he would a better one too.

~*~

"Do you feel as if you did the right thing?" Kip had gone to see Danburn as soon as he finished getting things set up for Kenneth. "He could fuck it all up and return, only to hold something more over your head."

"He could, but I don't think he will. I had Cassie with me when I was talking to him. She...I guess you could call it channeled in on him, saw his thoughts and what was in his heart. I also covered him so that he'd have clothing and money. Each of the next things I gave to him were things that he had to pass a test for. Not thinking of just himself for the money. Then when he was in the line at the store, he only had to get things that would be for a trip. He purchased cheap clothing, most of it on the clearance rack. Kenneth didn't purchase things that he could have in the store, such as guns and ammo. I didn't give him his tears back, not that I thought I could. Nor did I tell him where to go. He took a bus, not a plane, also saving money like he should have all along."

"I will have to take something from you, so that when I go to the other board members I can tell them that I have taken care of the fines for you, and that as far as I'm concerned, you did the right thing." Kip asked Danburn if he thought that he had. "The only person that can answer that is you. If you feel like this was the right thing to do, then I will stand beside you on it. You're a smart man, and one that has been hurt by them before. If you were to have come to me about it first, I would have told you no. Again, you did the right thing in that, but don't ever do it again. All right?"

"Yes, all right." Danburn asked him if he had anything of value on him. "Yes, the most treasured thing that I could think of. I thought that you'd want something that meant a great deal to me, so I brought it."

Handing over the deed to the house that he and Dalton lived in, he laid it on the desk. Danburn took it, read it over, and handed it back. Kip asked him if it wasn't good enough. He wasn't sure what else he had.

"Consider this a wedding gift, Kip." Kip wasn't sure the council was going to go for that, and told his friend that. "You gave it to me willingly, and I know how much the house means to the two of you. I'm assuming that you spoke to Dalton about this? What did she say?"

"Dalton told me to bring this to you, that this meant the world to her as well, and that if you had a problem with it, she'd come here and show you how much it was costing us by taking it out of your hide. I think she was sort of hoping that you'd not take it." Danburn laughed and asked what she thought about the help he gave to Kenneth. "She said she was proud of me. That she loved me too."

Danburn looked at him. Kip wasn't worried. He didn't have anything more precious than the deed to their home that he was willing to part with. Dalton was the most wonderful thing he'd ever had given to him, but he'd rather go to prison than to give her away. Plus, he was sure that Danburn would bring her back after a couple of hours. Dalton would make his life hell if he spent more than that amount of time with her.

As he was walked back to his home, he wondered if Kenneth would be able to do it. Cassie said that he would, and Carmine called him not two seconds after he talked to Cassie and told him that Kip's brother would be all right. That he'd get a job and would, whenever he could, tell people that his brother had provided him with a new outlook on life. It wasn't what he'd thought about when he helped his brother. But it did make him feel good that it had meant so much to him.

"Did he take it?" Kip told Dalton what Danburn had said. "I knew he'd come around for us. I've been thinking about your brother. What do you suppose really made him come to you? I mean, it wasn't guilt. As you said, he didn't apologize for anything. So what do you think it was?"

"He might not have said the words to me, but I really think he regretted the way things turned out. Not just for me, but for all of them." Dalton asked if he had mentioned his sister getting the same deal. "No, now that you mention it. He didn't ask about Mom and Dad either. He didn't ask for this; I offered and he took it. If you want to know if I'll do the same for the others, no, I won't. Not even if they find out about him. Which, when a dragon offers you freedom, it means that all ties that you had before are broken. The only person that he can ever speak to again is me. No one from his past will ever have any connection to him again. He won't be able to have any contact with anyone now that he's gotten his freedom, to assure that it doesn't get back to his past acquaintances. That would mean family too."

"I didn't know that. Kenneth gave up a great deal to do this, didn't he?" Kip nodded. "No wonder you were willing to help him after he had agreed. I don't know that I'd have been able to do that. Perhaps before, but not now. Not since I met you guys."

"Me either. I was thinking of that when I was coming back here. How much you mean to me. How much I love you." She hugged him and then held onto him. "Dalton, when we get out of here later today, I want to make this the most amazing Christmas ever. It'll be our first together, and we'll have lots more."

"That sounds wonderful." They had finished packing up last night when they got back. Today they were all meeting for breakfast, then going on to the airport. Dalton looked at him as she put her things in the car. "Do you suppose that we can find something for our staff? They've been getting to know us as much as we them. I'd like to do that."

"I think that's an excellent idea. We'll make a list of them while we fly so we don't miss anyone." Kip thought about all the things that he'd ordered online, and hoped that the staff did what he asked and put them in one of the empty bedrooms. "By the way, I was wondering if you had any decorations to put on the tree that the faeries put up for us? Anything from your childhood or after you left home?"

"I don't have anything but a tiny little ceramic tree that for the most part I forget to light up when I was there. Which honestly wasn't all that often anyway." Dalton leaned back in the seat and laid her head on his shoulder. "Do you suppose that after we deal with your parents we can start to have a normal life?"

"I haven't any idea what normal really is, do you?" She laughed with him. "We'll do the best we can. When we get back home, we'll start to work on that baby. Dragons have to have sex six times a day to conceive. You were told that, weren't you?" She eyed him as if she knew he was pulling her leg. When she told him to behave, he closed his eyes. "I had to give it my best shot, you know."

Sleeping off and on to their destination, he thought about what he wanted to do today—have fun, and not think about his family. Yes, he thought, that would be the best thing for this trip. Just to enjoy the day.

Chapter 7

"I told you six times already, I don't know where Kenneth is." Bethany reached out for her brother once again and got nothing. "He's not dead, is he? That would be just like you to not tell me that he died."

"How would he have died, you moron? He's a fucking dragon. Besides, the last person to see him was your mother and I. We certainly didn't kill him. He'd gone up to bed, and that was the last time we spoke to him. He never said a word about leaving. Even if he did leave here, why didn't he take the car?" Her dad looked at Mom. "Did he seem a little upset before he went up? I mean, he did talk about some crazy shit. Get this. He didn't want to go with me to rob us a bank so we'd have some money. You think that he went there on his own and did it?"

"No. I don't think so. We would have heard about it on the news, don't you think?" Bethany rolled her eyes at her mother's statement. Her parents were idiots. Worse than that, they thought they were smarter than anyone, including her and Kenneth. "Bethany, when you had the encounter with that woman, the queen of us, did she say anything about

Kenneth?"

"No, Mother. Why would she? It's not like she knew him at all. Not to mention, she wasn't likely to know that he was out of prison yet, now was she?" The woman, she forgot her name, had told Bethany that she'd have to report to her husband. Not fucking likely, she thought. Then she looked at her parents. "Have you guys been to see the king of dragons yet? I guess you were supposed to report to him when you got here."

"I have no intention of bowing down before a man like Danburn. His father caused us a great deal of trouble over the years. I mean, he's the one that had our tears taken from us." Father huffed. "It's none of their business how we treat our children. Nor how we discipline them. Fucking nosey bastard. Did you know that he took Kip to see the council every time he ran to see them? Like he was his father or something."

"That's one of the reasons that I hated Kip so much. He always thought that he was better than us because he hung out with Danburn. He was a know it all too. Kip would have been better off if we'd just smothered him like we had plans to. Then we'd not have all this trouble." Bethany looked at the meal that her mother set down in front of her. "What is this? It looks like shit."

"Yes, I'm serving you shit now. I have to go in after your father every day and get it for you." Mother huffed at her. "It was in the freezer. I didn't read all the words on the package. I just followed the instructions."

"You mean you didn't read the pictures?" Her mother hit her in the face with the pot she had in her hand that had something else mushy in it. That, of course, started a fight between them, and it wasn't until her father hit both of them that they stopped. "She started it."

"Yes, now look where your fighting with your mother

has gotten us. The kitchen is a mess." It was too. Not only was the table broken, but the stove was turned on its side as well as the door ripped from the refrigerator. "We'll have to find us another place to live now. I swear, we need to make it to the castle so we can have our own things back."

The knock at the door startled all of them into quietness. They had been worried about this since they killed the couple who had lived here and taken over their home. It was an okay house, really, but Bethany, like her parents, wanted the castle back. Father answered the door on the second knock.

"I have a letter here for Steven Newton." Father corrected the young man that he was Lord Newton. "If you say so. You need to sign for this."

After Father made his x, all he could manage even for as old as he was, the man handed him the envelope and turned and walked away. Father handed it over to her and she tore the envelope in half. Father asked her what the hell she was doing.

"Do you really want to know? I mean, who, besides Kenneth, knows that we live here? No one. So whoever knows that we're here, they aren't going to be giving us good news." Father picked up the envelope and told her to read it. "All right. But don't say that I didn't warn you."

Bethany read it over twice before looking at her parents. They were in deeper shit than she'd thought when she'd torn the letter into pieces. Father asked her what it said three times before she was able to speak.

"It's from Danburn Fletcher. The man has more titles than all of us put together. We're to go to his place of business and have good reason why we haven't come to tell him that we're residing here. Also, he said that we're to make amends for the death of the humans, as well as any damages to their home." Bethany then read the rest of it, not wanting to see the look on their faces when she read it out loud, paraphrasing the last two paragraphs so they'd understand. "We have no rights to the castle. That we forfeited those when we destroyed it and the grounds surrounding it. He also says that Kenneth will not be a part of this family ever again, and that there is never going to be contact with him. He's been given his freedom."

"Freedom? Who would do that to him? And why would our son take it? Surely that's a mistake. He'd never do anything like that, leaving no way for us to contact him." Bethany didn't mention that he had done it and it was a done deal; she was so hurt by him leaving her that she didn't speak. "I want you to get in touch with Kenneth right now. Call out to him and see if this is true."

"It's true. None of us have been able to contact him for a couple of days now. It's gotta be true or we would have been able to speak to him." Bethany laid her head on the couch back and let the tears flow. "He's left me. Just up and left me like we didn't have this special connection."

"It's a lie." Bethany looked at her father, hopeful that he knew something that she didn't. "They killed him, that's what it is. The council has killed him and are now hiding it from us so we won't be upset. I know that's what happened."

"What about going to see Danburn? We have to, you know. I don't want to, but I'm betting that if we don't then hell will be paid." Bethany knew that Danburn wouldn't kill them. He was supposed to be this really nice guy, and wouldn't take anything else from them. "You know, I'm going to ask him about Kenneth too. He's hidden him away someplace, and I'll get to the bottom of this right now."

They were all suppose to go, but Father said that he'd handle it on his own. That was fine with her and her mother. She no more wanted to go see the man than she did to have her dragon caught in a net. No, she wanted nothing to do with the other man.

Dad dressed up and left them. He was gone for no more than twenty minutes or so when there was another knock at the door. She nearly pissed her pants when she opened the front door to find not just the queen there that she'd met up with a week or so ago, but a couple of dozen guards there with her.

"You were told to come to the meeting. I'm very sure that should have been very clear to you all." The guard put iron shackles around their necks and escorted them to the door. As they were leaving, the queen spoke again. "You are in deep shit here. I hope you've made no plans for the rest of your short life."

"Where is my son?" Bethany wanted to warn her mother to shut up about him, but she asked several more times where Kenneth was. "You've imprisoned him, haven't you? That is the worst thing you could do to me. I love my son more than anything in this world. His sister too. You have no right to take him from me."

"What about Kip? Isn't he your son too?" Mother huffed and tilted her nose up in the air. "I see. No use for him, I'm guessing. Well, that's good. I don't think him or his new bride have any use for you either. Have you tried to get into the castle? I can only assume that you've not. You'd be badly burned had you tired. I wish you had, to be honest with you. Having the three of you incapacitated would suit everyone just fine and dandy, I think."

"Why, you upstart of a woman. You cannot speak to me that way." Bethany tried to get her mom to shut up, this was the king's mate, but she was talking faster now. "You get out of our home this moment. I don't know who the hell you think you are, but you're no longer welcome in this house. And you will take theses restraints off this moment. Don't think that I won't tell the king of this when I see him either."

"I'm his wife. Queen of the dragons. You are starting to piss me off more than when I was asked to come here and get you." She crossed her arms over her chest and Mother stepped back. "Get in that van right now, or so help me, I'll make what Danburn is going to do to you look like child's play."

The ride to the building was made in silence. There wasn't even a sound coming from the engine or the armed men with them. Bethany wondered if her father was having any more luck in getting them out of this than they were. Doubtful. Father was as dumb as a bushel of potatoes.

They were put into more irons when they arrived, and put into different cells in the sublevels of the building. She wanted to talk to her mother, tell her what she knew, but couldn't speak. They'd been forbidden. Even with that, she was sure that some magic had taken away their ability to speak to each other through their link anyway. Whoever these people thought they were, they had some pretty powerful magic.

"Felicia Newton, come stand before the king."

Bethany asked the man there if she was going as well. Her mother was again chained, this time around her ankles too.

"Shut up before I shut you up," the man barked at Bethany.

Bethany started to speak then. He turned to her and shifted from the waist up. Startled, Bethany screamed and fell back when the biggest wolf she'd ever seen snapped at her. In that moment she realized that she was in deep shit. It was a Canon wolf. Bethany would bet anything that he was the leader of the pack, Shawn Canon. Not just the oldest of all wolves, but the very first shifter of them as well.

Sitting on the floor, the only place afforded to her to do so, she thought about her fate. Bethany was going to ask to be set free too. There wasn't anything that Kenneth did that she'd not done. If someone would ask her, she'd tell them that she was a better dragon than he was too. Whoever gave him the freedom, they'd have to give it to her as well. She wasn't going to stand before this man and be judged on things that were none of his business.

It seemed like hours since her mother was taken away. Bethany was also worried that she'd not seen her father since they arrived. Things had to be going well, she told herself. They had let the two of them go, so she would be as well.

"Or perhaps they blamed everything on you, and now you're in here for the rest of your days." Bethany hated talking to herself, but there wasn't anyone to listen to her right now. "Freedom. I'm going to ask for freedom the first thing, before he opens his mouth. That way I can't be judged by anyone, and I can go away too. Start all over with Mother and Father. And once I find Kenneth, we'll be one big happy family again."

Bethany must have fallen asleep, because when she woke up, the room was dark and she could only see as far as her hand would reach in front of her. She realized that it had been hours too, by the way that she felt. Her body was stiff and cold, and she was sure that it had been a long time since she'd eaten. Wishing now that she had her purse with her, Bethany thought about the stash of food she had in it. At least her belly wouldn't think her throat had been sliced open and no food could pass.

Time had no meaning for her as she waited on some word that her parents were all right. No one came to her either when the sun started to shine from someplace in the hall in front of her. Now she could see that there were eight other cells across from her. Bethany did wonder if all of them were full. There was something decidedly wrong going on, and she was afraid that the longer they waited to come and get her, the more she was going to have to suffer at this almighty king's hand.

About the time she was ready to give up on any hope of anyone coming for her, thinking that they'd forgotten about her, the same man who had taken her mother away came for her. Bethany was shaking so badly by then, fear of the unknown making her a little jumpy, that she went with Mr. Canon without a word. Whatever had happened to her parents, she was sure that they'd not do the same to her. She was, after all, their child, and had no control over their actions.

The room was full of people. Humans were in with the shifters. Most of them were wolves, but there were a great number of dragons as well. The three men that sat up on the raised platform seemed to have just shared a joke. All thoughts of her blaming everything on her parents flew out the window, along with her fear.

"What the fuck do you find so fucking funny? You've had me locked up for hours without a single meal, and now I come in here and you're making fun of me. What sort of shit are you conducting in here? I want you to give me my freedom too. My brother was much worse than I was, and I want you to give me what he has. Or better yet, take it from him and give whatever he has to me. I'm the nicer of the two of us."

She huffed when told to sit. Before she could refuse, however, she was shoved down into the iron chair and shackled to it. The burn of the metal hurt her everywhere it touched her.

"Bethany Newton. My goodness, you have a long list of things that you've done. Before you spout off about how you were only doing what your parents told you, that will not fly at all. These misdeeds of yours, mostly done out of meanness and not anything more, were done all on your own." She didn't say anything, wanting Danburn to get to the point. "By the way, you will not be getting freedom, not in the way that you wish. Nor will anyone take anything from your brother. What was given to Kenneth was a one-time deal, and he is doing very well with it."

"So? Are you saying that I can't do as well as, if not better than, him? That would be a lie. I'm a very good person." She noticed Kip getting up from a seat that was just behind her. "Whatever he has to say, no one wants to hear it. Especially me. He's been nothing but a pain in the ass for as long as I've known him. Ask my parents if you don't believe me. Where are they, anyway?"

"Paying their debts. Kip, go ahead with what you wanted to say against your sister." She screamed for him to shut up, but Danburn had someone put a mask over her face. If she opened her mouth again, the iron would slip into her body and she'd be dead soon. "Now, as I was saying, what is it you have to say against your sister, Kip?"

"When I was only one hundred and twelve years old, much too young to be put out of the family home, I was thrown out by not just my sister, but my parents as well. I didn't know what the reasoning for that was until later. Bethany had wanted the room that I had, because it looked down over the citizens of the town where we lived. She loved, she told me later, looking down on people beneath her. To Bethany everyone was beneath her." She wanted to scream at him that it wasn't her fault that he had the best view of the town. Not to mention, she didn't like him in the house with them in the first place. "After I was thrown out of the house, she destroyed everything that was mine. Even books that I had been lent from Lord Fletcher, Danburn's father."

She was asked what she had to say for that, and the mask was taken off her face. "He had the nicest room in all the

101

castle. He kept his room girly clean, and even his bed was made every day. I liked that it was really nice. You should have seen it after I was there for a month." Bethany laughed. "I couldn't even get the faeries that were there before me to clean up after me anymore, it was so bad."

"Did you take pride in the fact that you had what he no longer did?" She said that she had, as a matter of fact. "Then you willfully destroyed his things for no other reason than you could."

"Sure. Why not? No one liked him anyway." Bethany realized that she couldn't lie to the people at the table. Danburn smiled at her when she said that. "Have you given me some sort of drug or magic to make it so that I cannot lie to you? That's totally unfair, if you ask me."

"I didn't, but you will tell the truth or go back to your cell. You'll answer the questions anyway, Bethany, but you can do it here or from your cell; that is entirely up to you." She had no answer to that, so closed her mouth. Just as the mask was going back on, she asked where her parents were. "None of that is your concern. You just continue to answer the questions."

The mask was put back on her face in seconds. The entire time that Kip talked about everything she'd done to him, she would only have the mask off for moments to say if she'd done it or not. Honestly, there was nothing on his list that she'd not done to him. In fact, some of them she hadn't thought of in years.

So it went on. For hours she was asked to verify things that she'd done. Things that she and her parents had done to him together, or even to some humans. Her only response to those questions was why wasn't she able to do whatever she wanted to humans. They were nothing more than dinner to her and her parents.

No one said anything about Kenneth being in on some of her schemes. They never mentioned how when she'd tied up Kip and set him on fire, Kenneth was there with her, egging her on. Even when she mentioned him, bringing him in on some of the meanness, they called it, against Kip, those words were stricken from the record, as he had freedom.

"Why am I not having my freedom? Or is this your way of working up to it? I don't care for the way you're doing this, if that's where this is leading. I want whatever you gave to Kenneth. It's my right as the only female child of Steven and Felicia Newton." Kip asked her what rights she thought that she had. "The right to kill you when this is finished, you backstabbing shit ass. What makes you think that when this is all over and they slap me on the wrist that I'm not going to make your life more of a living hell than I did before?" She realized in that second that she'd fucked up. "I was only joking, Your Honor, or whatever you are. It's just siblings teasing each other. Isn't that right, Kip?"

"You have never once, in all my life, done anything remotely like a joke or teased me. You only knew one thing, Bethany. That was to threaten me, then carry out those threats with a promise. You were and still are the worst part of my life, the one person that I feared more than death itself." She told him he was joking. "No, I am not. I will be the happiest man in the world when I know for a fact that you are out of my life."

The three men talked quietly amongst themselves. She couldn't make out what they were saying, but they stared at her a great deal while they talked. Surely, Bethany thought, they'd let her go on principle. She hadn't done anything wrong to any other dragon that she knew.

"Bethany Newton, you will stand and hear your sentence."

She stood up and smiled at the men there. Whatever was

coming, she knew that she was going to have enough of her time left to get back to Kip and make him regret keeping notes on shit that she'd done to him.

~*~

Felicia didn't care for this sort of work. Nor did she think that she should have received the same sentencing that her husband had. Steven was a man, and therefore suited more to the labor that they were made to do. Now that Bethany was here, she felt too that she, as a younger dragon, should be made to take up her slack and be kinder to her. But then Bethany hadn't been kind to anyone, as far as she knew.

The slap of an iron covered whip hit her across the back. Her dragon was hurting from all this shit she'd been made to do. But the alternative was much worse, and she certainly wasn't going to give up her dragon to live out the rest of her days.

"Get to work." Her dragon shied away from the whip when it hit her again. Being made to use her fire to dry out the mud that had nearly been a mudslide on a village below was demeaning to her. But she knew better than to say a word now that she knew what the punishment was to do so. Looking around again, she tried to find Steven. He had been gone far too long, she thought.

"Why did you tell them that I was the meanest person that you knew?" Bethany again. Every time there was a small lull in what they were supposed to be doing, Bethany would ask her about something from her trial. Did she think that they had gotten off Scott free? No, they hadn't. "Mother, I'm speaking to you, and you'll answer me."

Smack. Felicia felt the sting of the whip as it hit her again. But when they hit Bethany twice more than she'd gotten, that made her sting feel not quite so bad.

"Stop fucking hitting me. That wasn't anything that I

104

was suppose to receive for coming here." The big man hit her again, then again. "You'll stop that right now, or I'll turn my fire onto you. Then what will you do with your iron against me? Nothing, I'll tell you. Because you'll be fucking dead."

This went on for an hour. Bethany would stop working and then the man would hit her. She could tell that it was making her weaker and weaker, the whip hitting Bethany. But no amount of telling her to shut up and behave would make her lessen her beating. This was a nightmare. But she'd work it until this job was finished. That was hers and Steven's punishment. They would work until there was no more work needed from them.

When the whistle was blown for them to stop for their meal, Felicia wanted to be the first in line to get something to eat. But true to form, not only was Bethany first in line, but she'd knocked over several other dragons to get there.

Bethany was pulled out of the line, and Felicia thought it was funny how much Bethany was in trouble here. It seemed to take the focus off of her for a while. She supposed she shouldn't think such horrible thoughts about her own child, but she thought that between Steven, Kenneth, and Bethany, they had caused the most trouble for her. Felicia's defense was that she didn't want to be left behind. That wasn't going to happen again, she'd been told. By no less than the king and queen.

Wondering what she'd do after this, how they would live their lives out, Felicia thought about all the places that she wanted to live. They were forbidden to take a home from someone that was living in it. Also, and this upset her more than anything, they were never to breach the castle that had been in their family for generations. Like they had no rights to it. She'd just see about that. Sitting down with her meal, she was glad that they made them eat as humans. There was nothing on her plate that would have satisfied her dragon. It didn't do much for her either.

Felicia figured there was about an hour or so more work to be done here and she'd be free. The man that had hit her with the whip came around with a sheet of paper that he was handing out to everyone else. When she was ordered to take hers, she read that her next assignment was to go to another place and do the same thing. Dry out the mud and then put it on the lower levels of the valley for gardening.

"Excuse me. This isn't mine." He just stared at her as she tried to return it to him. "This isn't mine. After this job, I was told that I could be free."

"Oh yeah. Did you notice anything about me that looks like I give a crap? No. And you know why? Because I don't. Your name is on the list to work until there was no more work for you." She nodded, telling him that was right. "This is considered work. So therefore, you're going to work. Until there is no more work for you to do."

"I don't understand this. Danburn said that we were to be free after there was...." Felicia sat down on the ground again. "After there was no more work for us. I don't suppose you know how long that will be, do you?"

He walked away laughing. Felica sat there, looking at the paper that she'd been handed. She knew that she'd be doing this for the rest of her days, and beyond. Working for humans to save their lives.

Getting up, she moved to where the mud was and stared at it. Mud and dirt. She felt like it was in every one of her pores. All over her body, like she'd been made of it. This was no way for a lady of the castle to be treated. Not at all.

As the mud began to slide again, something that she was used to, instead of drying it out, she moved closer to it. Anyone, she thought, would wonder what she was doing, but it was much too late for them to pull her loose. Letting the mud take her under its coil of death, Felicia reached out for Steven and told him how much she loved him, but that she was unable to do this sort of work any longer.

As the mud took her breath away, she allowed herself one more thought. She was going to be a dead dragon, but a very happy one.

Chapter 8

Kip sat on the deck of the hotel room, completely oblivious to the cold, watching the snow coming down to the hotel lawn. His mother was dead. Not sure how he felt about that, he just sat there thinking of all the times that he'd wished her so. Kip didn't have any love for his family, but knowing that she'd taken her own life, he did wonder why she'd done it.

"Are you all right?" Kip took Dalton's hand into his and held it when she spoke. "I didn't think she'd been doing the work for all that long. Steven said that she told him she could no longer do that sort of work."

"She'd been doing it for less than two days. Not nearly long enough for her to have gotten the hang of it, much less sick of the job." Dalton told him what else she'd heard from the job site. That his mom had thought that she'd be done at the end of the day and free to go. "Yes, Danburn told me about it. I guess she thought she was above all that. Father said that it was my fault too."

"Of course he did. Did you hear that he had to go and see to a wound that was on his leg before going back to work? Denny, the foreman, said that it was self-inflicted, and that

Steven only needed to shift and it would have been okay. I guess he refused in the event that there was something in the mud that would ruin his body. Whatever that meant." Kip laughed when Dalton snorted about his father. "Also, Bethany has been given the rest of the day off to deal with her pain. It sounded to me like she was more pissed off at her mother than grieving over her dying. She's to pick up the extra work from her parents. I guess that isn't going over well."

"No, it wouldn't." Kip got up when Dalton did. "I guess we should go inside. Sitting out here isn't going to help me to understand what was going through her head when she slipped into the slide."

"No. More than likely no one will ever understand why she did it."

As soon as they entered the hotel room, Danburn was there. He'd said that he was coming to their room to talk, but not about what.

After having room service bring them some drinks and a tray of scones hot from the oven, Danburn said that he needed to talk to Dalton, but he wanted Kip to be there. After he finished off nearly all the scones and cold tea, he leaned back and looked at Dalton.

"I don't know that this is a good idea or not, but it's already done and you have to deal with it." In that moment, Kip knew what was going on. He smiled when he thought of what Dalton might say to them when she figured it out. "You're going to have to come to me and pledge yourself to me. That'll be all I demand of you, with you being family and all."

"What the fuck are you talking about? Have you been up all night again with the baby? You deserve it, even if she's not puked on your shoulder yet." Danburn laughed. "What? Get to the point, you asshole. Why would I have to pledge myself

110

to you at all?"

"Your dragon does." She just stared at Danburn, then at Kip. "You've received the dragon of Felicia. She's a little touchy about how she was treated, but both Kendrick and I think that if anyone can handle her, you can do it."

"I don't understand. What do you mean, my dragon has to do this?" When she didn't get an answer from Danburn, she looked at him. "Kip? What is he talking about?"

"I didn't know this until lately. But when the human side of a dragon dies, the dragon is left behind and goes someplace that is familiar and safe to them. Not that I'd think there are too many places for my mother's dragon, but that is where she went, I guess." Dalton looked ready to explode, so he hurried up with what he was speaking about. "A dragon needs a host. Danburn thought, and I agree with him, that you should get one of the dragons that were my family's. My brother has one too, but when I gave him his freedom, I didn't take his dragon. But with Mother being dead, her dragon needed you. As her host."

"She *needed* me?" Kip nodded. "Are you telling me that I have her dragon now? That she's with me?"

"Yes. But I need to tell you a few things. She's hurt. Not physically, but she's hurt like you were from the things done to you. That's why I thought that you'd be the prefect host for her." Dalton asked him what he meant. "Well, for one thing, she's been mistreated. Her tears were taken from her as well. I'm sure that she understands that it was because of the abuse that was set upon her. But to be honest with you, Dalton, I don't know what she'll need from you to be a dragon that you can call upon."

"You mean she might just let me die." He didn't think it would come to that, but he just didn't know and told her so. "I see. Do you know how I can make her trust me?"

"No. I know, however, that you can do it. You're strong enough to have survived your own family and the way that they treated you." She started pacing the room. "I can have Danburn take her back. You'd never miss her because you've only just found out that she's there."

"I've known for an hour, I think. I kept feeling this...I guess this movement over me that was sort of strange. Does she have a name?" Kip told her that his didn't, but that didn't mean that they couldn't have their own relationship. "I'll need time, then. To make her a part of my life before I call to her."

"I'd say that she'd more than likely not come to you right now. Mother could only bring her when she commanded her to come. When they were working, it was said that she would have a hard time just getting her to do anything for her. Mostly only then because of the whip that the wolves used on them to make them work. I'm not positive, but I believe that the dragon left her before my mother died."

"So she's hurt and scared. I can feel that part of her. It explains my mood today. Also, she's not very trusting, is she?" Kip said that he would imagine not. "Okay. I have my work cut out for me, but I'll have her trusting me. She might not ever save me, but I'd very much like for her to trust me."

"As I said, if you wish to have her taken away, I can—" Dalton cut him off. Shaking her head, she told him that she was hers and that she wanted her there. "She might prove to be too much, Dalton. I want you to know that if she is, then we can take her away."

"Then what will happen to her?" He didn't answer her, hoping that he'd not have to say the words to her. "She'll never be with another person, will she? She won't be free to fly in the skies as she should."

"No, she won't." Nodding, Dalton left him there and moved out to the deck that was on the twentieth floor of their hotel. She would be warm enough there. Even if the dragon didn't want to warm Dalton, she would want herself to be warm. He spoke to Danburn through their link so he'd not alarm Dalton. *I'm worried about her. Dalton may need her, and the dragon won't come for her.*

Kip, I think that if anyone can save the dragon, it'll be Dalton. They're a great deal alike. They only need to figure that out. The dragon will soon learn that Dalton is strong enough to give her what she wants. Of that I'm sure. But, and this is what I want you to know, if she doesn't save Dalton when she needs it, I will destroy the dragon.

Danburn could, and would too. He was much stronger than anyone knew, even himself. Kip was also sure that Danburn had magic within himself that he'd never used, and would be surprised to know that he even had it. He was the king for that and many other reasons. Also, Danburn was well loved, and to Kip that was the strongest and purest magic of all. Love.

~*~

"I want you to be safe and secure." Dalton talked to her dragon while she stood on the grounds of the hotel, looking at the decorations around the beautifully decorated area. "I also want for you to be loved, and for you to know that you're loved."

Nothing. She didn't figure that she, her dragon, would speak to her, but she would tell her what she wanted from her. Nothing but friendship. Perhaps for her to save her when she needed it. But it was more important to her that the dragon feel that Dalton was never going to order her around, nor would she abuse her in any way.

"I never even had a pet when I was younger. Not that I think of you as my pet, but just someone that would comfort me. In this case, however, I'd like nothing more than to give

113

you comfort. I've only heard a few things about Felicia, my mate's mother, but I know that she'd not be anyone that I'd like to hang out with." The warmth from within her took the coldness away from her. "Thank you for that. I don't know if it was for my benefit or not, but I do thank you for warming me up."

You cannot know the suffering that I had. Dalton sat down. Her dragon's voice was so harsh, like it had never been used before. *I have never spoken to her. She did not heed what I said to her when it came to being safe. And because of that, I now have to contend with you.*

"No, you don't. You can leave me this very moment should you want. I'd understand." The dragon told her that she only said those words. "Should you like, I can go to Danburn now and have him take you from me."

You lie. Instead of being upset, she called out to Danburn and asked him to come to her. Dalton wasn't sure that the dragon knew that could be done, but when he landed in the hotel yard as his great dragon, she told him what the dragon wanted.

She knows what will happen to her should she not stay with you? Dalton told Danburn that she didn't know, but more than likely the dragon knew. *I'm sure that she does. Tell her that she must come from your body as she did Felicia's, and I will destroy her.*

"Is that what you wish? To be destroyed rather than staying with me? Then you should do it now before I get too much more used to you being here." The dragon said nothing as Dalton spoke. Danburn, shifting to his human part, waited with her. "I don't know what you are called, but I would like to call you something besides Dragon."

I am Nothing. That is what I was called. Dalton told her that that wouldn't do. *You called the great king to come here and*

114

destroy me.

No, I called Danburn here at your request to leave my body. You will have to face the consequences of what that brings you. As I said, I'd like for you to remain with me. I certainly don't want you destroyed. But if that is your wish, then I want nothing for you but what you want. Dragon said nothing again, and Dalton looked at Danburn. "I don't think she even wants to try and get to know me. That really breaks my heart."

"I know, love. You are a tender person when you wish to be. Hell on wheels when you need to be. It is why I thought you could make it work with her." Dalton nodded and asked the dragon again what she wanted to do. "Please tell her that this is her wish that I am doing for her. No one will force her to do anything."

I heard him. It is true of you. You are much too tender to live out your life without a keeper. Dalton smiled and told her that was why she had Kip. *Kipling is a good man. His dragon is my son.*

"I never thought of it that way. Yes, he is. We're going to have children soon too. They'd be your grandchildren." The dragon moved over her skin. While it wasn't painful, it wasn't very comfortable either. "Are you leaving me? If so, please know that I shall miss you. Nor will I want another dragon. That isn't blackmailing you, but I will forever feel as if I failed you, and I don't want to do that again."

You have not failed me. My host, she did that all on her own. Dalton told her she was sorry, and felt the pain of the dragon stretching her body. *I am a great and powerful dragon. Should I wish, I could tear you apart and never think a thing about it.*

"Yes, I suppose you could. I don't want you to, that's the truth of it. But if you want to destroy me so that you can feel justified about leaving me, then I guess there is little I can do about it." Dalton thought of something. "I would like to point out that Danburn has plans of taking your mate's dragon from his host, and that of your daughter. Your other son — I'm sorry, I don't know his name either, the one that Kenneth has — is with a better man than Kenneth was before. He's been given his freedom, and that of his dragon. They have moved on, are going to be a great man and dragon. I know from a friend of mine that they're already paying it forward on the gift that they received by helping other dragons deal with the families that they were born to. He is a good man. And because of his dragon, he will be a great man. Danburn is waiting, my lady Dragon. Go in peace."

I will see how you work out. Dalton told Danburn what she'd said to her. *You are nothing like my other host. You are somewhat of a sap.*

"I've been called worse. If you stay, will you talk to me whenever I speak to you? You don't have to. I'm not ordering you to do so, but I would so like to have a friend to talk to on occasion."

I do not wish to be your friend, Lady Newton. I will be here should you wish it, but I cannot befriend you. I do not trust you at all. Dalton was hurt by the sting of her words, but told her that she understood. *We have that settled. Now I wish to rest. It is hard on a dragon to be shifted from one to another host. Do not bother me.*

"She doesn't like me." Dalton sat down next to Danburn, and he wrapped his arm around her to keep her warm. "I don't think that she'll ever trust me not to hurt her, either."

It was too much. They were set to leave day after tomorrow, Christmas Eve, and she had a lot of shopping to do. The list had grown so much that she was fearful that they'd have to rent a second plane to take it all home. Telling Danburn thanks for helping her out, she watched as he got rid of the prints his dragon had left in the snow. It was funny the things that she never thought of in keeping a dragon safe.

Kip met her at the largest toy store she'd ever seen. Helping Elissa buy toys and other things for the pack had been so much fun that she went a little overboard with the gifts to the children of their staff. For the staff too, if she was truthful.

"I think we should get a few things for the house. I know that the faeries have given us a wonderful home to live in, but I think we need something that we picked out on our own." She asked Kip about the big television. "Well, that was a necessity. You know that."

They had fun. Every once in a while she'd feel the dragon moving over her. It was a good feeling now that she knew what it was, but her heart still hurt for her lack of trust. Dalton went to the bathroom while Kip paid for the items that they'd gotten for their house.

Don't move out of the stall yet. Locking the door that she'd just unlocked, Dalton did what she'd been told. *You are in trouble, my lady.*

All right. Okay. I'm not sure what I should do. Bring Kip in? She was told not yet; he would be harmed as well. *Why me?*

The man sent a woman in to kill you for your ring and money. He has noticed how you are spending money and that you carry credit cards. We will deal with the woman. She asked if that meant killing her. *She has killed many before, my lady. Many more than I wish to talk about now.*

All right, but let's please make it quick. I don't want her to suffer needlessly. She could feel the dragon's laughter and decided to ignore it. Dalton was afraid. *What about the man? How will I deal with him?*

I have spoken to my son. He is speaking with Lord Kipling now. The woman was making noises like she was ill. *It is but a ruse. You are not to fall for it, my lady. Should you do so, then all will be lost.*

Don't you get hurt either, Lady Dragon. The dragon said that she'd not. *Good. I want you to be safe and unhurt. Just as I will be. Right?*

You will be safe if you listen to me. Should you think your plan is better than — Dalton told her she had no plan other than to be shaking in her shoes. *You are a strange human. You are aware of that, are you not?*

I'm afraid. That makes me strange? But as I said, Lady Dragon, you aren't to be harmed either.

When I tell you to do so, I wish for you to unlock the door. The noise will be covered when she — Now. She unlocked the stall door just as the woman got louder in her noise of puking. *She will come toward you now. Again, when I tell you, slam the door open as hard as you can, and hold it very tightly against the door of the stall she is in, just on the other side. You will hold her, then call for Lord Kipling.*

All right. Thank you so much. She said that she would do this for anyone. *I don't care who else you'd do this for, but I thank you for saving my ass.*

When it came time for her to slam the door back, she saw the gun skitter across the floor toward the wall. Dalton realized that she had more strength than she'd imagined, and was glad that the dragon was helping her. Calling to Kip, she was never so glad to see anyone than she was him in all her life.

Picking up the gun, Kip told her to let the door go. As soon as she did, the woman punched out, catching her on the jaw. As she was going down, she heard the gunshot and was so very happy for the help. Thanking the dragon over and over, Dalton hit her head on the floor and everything was just gone.

When she woke she was on one of the beds that was in

the store. Kip was holding her hand, but was barking orders to someone close to them. Whatever was going on, he was royally pissed off. Then she remembered.

Are you all right? The dragon seemed startled by the question. *You said that you'd be all right. I'm just making sure that you weren't hurt when I fell. I'm so terribly sorry about that. But I had no idea that I was going to fall.*

As I said, you are a strange person. You are no longer human, my lady. I have...I do not have as much trust in you as you do me, but I am beginning to allow you to grow on me. I have shared what I am with you. You are no longer a human, as I have said. Dalton thanked her. *I am all right. Lord Kipling is only making sure that there are no others in the store to harm others. He, the other man, is dead as well.*

Good. The slimy bastard nearly ruined our shopping trip. The dragon did laugh then. It was hardy and full. It also brought a smile to Dalton. That was when Kip looked at her. "I'm all right, I promise. My dragon, she saved me from being hurt and robbed."

"Thank you, Lady Dragon." The dragon said that she had a name. She told them both that she wished to be called Trust. "I love your pick of a name. Trust. It suits you both, I think. Dalton has too much, and you have very little. Perhaps one day you can decide that you balance each other out, and both of you can be safe."

The rest of the group showed up about ten minutes later. The police were taking statements and the bodies were being carried away. The store manager was so happy to have the would be robbers put out of commission that he thanked the two of them several times. The staff was much more helpful after that as well.

Dalton made sure that she was steady on her feet before she stood up. The wound at her head was healed, with just a tiny bit of a scar on her forehead. Kip told her that if she was to shift, it would disappear completely.

"I don't care if it does or not. I have my dragon, Trust, to thank for saving me, and it'll be a reminder of what she did for us both." Kip kissed her and they continued shopping. "I want to get my dragon something too. Do you know anything that a dragon would want? I'm being very serious about this."

"You'll have to talk to Danburn and see if he'll allow her to swim in his lake. It's very deep and full of fish. That would be about the only thing that I can think of that she'd enjoy." Dalton decided to talk to him about it later, and reached into her purse to get her notebook. Making notes was something that she did a great deal.

Pulling out what she thought was the notepad, she had in her hand a very beautiful scale. It was the purest of whites, and as shiny as the sun shining on the newly fallen snow. Turning her back to Kip, who was picking out something for their butler, she asked Trust where it had come from.

Should you kiss the scale, my lady, and then touch it to your belly, you will have a child of Lord Kipling's. It will be dragon, just as you are. She started to do that when Trust laughed again. *I should warn you that once you kiss the scale and hold it to your empty womb, you may have twins or more.*

I think I'd like that. Kissing the scale then putting it to her belly, she thought of the children that would come from this action. *Thank you so much, Trust. You'll see your grandchildren soon. How does that make you feel?*

Like I was brought to you for this very thing. Dalton cried, and when she wiped at her cheeks there were several gems, beautifully colored and large, in her hand. *I have my magic back, my lady. You gave me my magic of gems back. Thank you so much for that.*

She would have a child. Kip and her would be parents.

Thinking about that had her wandering over to the baby department and looking at all the things that she'd need. Some, she knew, would be pretty but not very useful. Picking up a small blanket that had a dragon on it, she thought of what Kip would say when he saw what she wanted.

Kip wrapped his arms around her from behind and kissed her neck. It was all it took to get her wet and ready for him. It seemed since they'd been together, there was never a day that passed that they didn't rip each other's clothing off and make love. Most of the time twice a day.

"I can smell you. You've had a gift from your dragon." Dalton told Kip what she'd done. "Christ, woman, are you trying your best to kill me? I mean, the thought of you round with our children makes me want to throw you to the floor and take you right now."

"You should know that you're not helping me. I think you need to find us a dark and very quiet place and — Where are we going?" Laughter from him and the dragon made her laugh as well. In less time than it took her to know that she wanted Kip's child as soon as possible, she was shoved into a broom closet and stripped of her clothing. Almost as soon as she was naked, Kip sat her on a stack of boxes and was kissing her. Dalton couldn't wait for him to fill her with his child.

~*~

Getting dressed was harder than he ever remembered it being. Not that he minded. Touching her, receiving kisses from her mouth was like tastes of heaven. When they made their way back out to the store they realized that it was later than they thought. The others had moved on to another floor to get other things for their group.

The little blanket was put away, and Kip snatched it up to buy for Dalton. It would be too soon for anyone to be able to smell that she was with child, but he'd know, and so would she. There were a lot of pieces to the layette set that he'd get later, but for now the blanket would keep them happy until they were able to share their happiness with the family.

By the time they made it back to the hotel, they only had a few minutes to get dressed and to the restaurant. They were excused for their tardiness because they'd all heard about the man and woman that they'd had the encounter with. Kip had forgotten all about it, and only missed a little of what they were saying when he thought about what he and Dalton had just done.

Created a child.

Chapter 9

Tomorrow was Christmas, and the festive lights and decorations were wonderful. Even the people working on this eve of all eves were in a great mood. Kip was able to get a few things that he loved for Dalton, and one for Elissa, the woman that had meant more than he could explain to her. Then after they had their celebration, they'd deal with his father and sister.

Neither of them were working out well at the job they'd been made to do. Father had been told about Mother, and of course he blamed that on Kip. Bethany refused to work anymore. She felt that she was to have a period of no less than one hundred years to mourn her mother's passing. All that she was allotted was two days. Kip thought that Danburn was being very generous with that. As far as he had been concerned, they should have both been put to death as soon as they were before him.

He supposed that it was cruel to want your family dead. Only he knew what they were actually like. How they had killed other people to get what they wanted. His father had gone on rampages and to the zoo or another park where animals were, and destroyed them simply for the pleasure of it. His sister, Bethany, had lured young children close to her, only to hurt them badly enough that they'd end up in the hospital. Several times they'd been killed by her when her temper got the better of her.

He'd heard from Kenneth that morning. Kip thought for sure that he was going to tell him that he couldn't do it. That not being able to be with his family was too much. It was against the rules that he'd set forth for him, but when he found out what Kenneth wanted, he was able to forgive him for his transgression.

I should like to ask a favor of you. Kip reminded him that he wasn't to contact him. *I know, but this is very important, Kip. I want you to never tell your children of me. I don't want you to think that I'm perfectly content now and you should name a child for me. I don't want that.*

Are you not content with what you're doing now? Kenneth cried then, and told him that he'd never been so happy, that he was doing the best that he could, and was enjoying his failures as well as being able to learn from them. *That's good to hear, Kenneth. I'm so very happy for you too.*

I have a job, Kip. One that pays me very little, but I like it. I work in a restaurant washing dishes. You'll be happy to know, too, that I have a friend. He's invited me to his home to meet his wife and family. I have never done that before. I don't even know what I should do. Kip asked him what he meant. *Should I bring a gift for them? I know that at one time that was the norm, but now, I have no idea. What would you do?*

Get some flowers for his wife and a basket of fruit for the household. Ask before you give the children anything, Kenneth, so that you don't harm them with food that they cannot eat, and be yourself. That is how he came to like you, and his family will too if you allow them to. He wanted to tell him not to hurt them, not to lose his temper and kill the family. But he didn't. Kip didn't want to give his brother anything bad to think about. *When you have a nice place of your own, remember the things that they did for you and you'll be able to invite all manner of people to your home.*

Kenneth thanked him and told him he was sorry for breaking the rules, but he had no one else to turn to but him. Kip told his brother that he was glad to be able to help him, and did tell him that he could do it again if he didn't make a huge habit of it. Kenneth thanked him several more times before the connection was closed.

The house was welcoming when they arrived home that night. The tree made it feel like they were walking into a Christmas store, it was so pretty. Dalton thought, after seeing all the ones on their trip, that theirs was the best. She took pictures of every little detail, telling him that she was going to have them to remember their first Christmas together. He only hoped that after dealing with his family that she'd still feel that way about it.

The staff was given their gifts, as well as money that they had put into pretty envelopes. It was a lot of money; he knew that, but they were loyal to them, and he wanted them to know how much they both were glad to have them. After handing out the gifts too, the staff was told to go home and enjoy Christmas with their own families. They were assured that the faeries were there to help out with any food that they might need.

After everyone had breakfast with Quinn and Hanson, they cleaned up and then met at Danburn's home for a day of fun, food, and friends.

Tomorrow his sister and father were going to be brought before Danburn, and Kip could tell that he was nervous about it. Not about what he had to do, but he thought it was how

Kip might react to it all. Kip decided to tell him right off what he felt about his family.

"As much as it pains me to say this, I want them dead." Danburn said that he'd been thinking about that too. "I know you have. I don't want you to worry about how I'm going to react to it. I want them out of my life, and death is the only way that is going to happen."

"Thank you." Kip nodded. "I've been asked to find someone else to be on the Board of Dragons with me. I would very much like for it to be you. You're a good man, and have a good heart. I think with the two of us working together, we can make a difference to so many lives."

"I don't know what to say." Danburn told him to say yes. "Of course I'll help you with the board. It would be an honor to work with you. Of course, I'll need to talk to Dalton about it."

"You mean because of the babies." Kip stared at him. "Yes, I can tell before anyone can. Being the king of dragons, you'd be amazed at all the crap that I know. Sometimes it's not so bad, but there are times when I'm overwhelmed by it all."

"I can well imagine." They both laughed as the game was found on the television. "By the way, don't sit next to Dalton when the game comes on. She can be slightly enthusiastic about bad calls. She doesn't even care which team it's on, she just gets really pissed off."

When the game was getting good, he noticed that Danburn had a pillow over his groin. He was either protecting it in case she hurt him, or he'd been hurt and was still trying to protect himself. Either way, it made him laugh.

Over the years, Elissa and Danburn had invited all the children from the local orphanage to their home to not just celebrate Christmas, but to get a good meal. They had all the kids over so that no one would feel slighted by the things that the other children might have gotten. So today they had nearly twenty children of varying ages with them. Kip was glad that Kendrick was all right with the tradition too.

Each of the families had been asked to give a donation to the cause. Elissa and all the women had gone shopping for the things that were needed by each child. Then they used what was left over, usually more donated by Danburn, to buy them toys or electronics. The older children, anywhere from twelve to seventeen, were as excited about those things as they were the big meal that they ate.

Presents had been given out to the adults at breakfast. The children were seated around the tree and waiting. It wasn't until Santa made an appearance that things started to get fun. Even the two babies, nearly a year old, were excited to see the big man in red.

"I want them." Kip asked Dalton who she was talking about. He thought the babies, but couldn't have been more wrong when she answered him. "The middle children. I want them all, but I don't think I'm equipped to handle seventeen children at once, and a dragon. What do you think?"

"We can take them all. With the faeries around, they'd be well cared for, as well as loved." She looked excited, then shook her head. "I was really hoping you'd say no. We are approved to take any children that you wish, love. Danburn made sure of that when the kids were invited here."

"I really would love to take the babies. Also the two twelve year olds. I think that Em and Dana are taking in the older three. To help them with college if they wish to go, and to make sure that they have a hand up when it comes to finding a place to live when they turn eighteen." He'd heard that Danburn and Kendrick were going to see about taking the two younger ones, both six from two different families.

"I'm going to talk to the other three. There isn't any reason that they couldn't take the other eight with them too."

By the end of the evening, not only did Hanson take four of the children back to his home, but Griff and Rette both took two. If they did this every year, Kip thought, there would be a house full every year for the rest of their lives. It occurred to him that he really didn't care, either.

~*~

Dalton wasn't sure how this worked. For a trial of dragons, they had to meet on the king's property. In that, it meant that they were in an open field with several large fires built up so that it was as warm as in their home. She supposed that having dragons keeping it warm, it would never burn out.

"I need to ask you a favor." Dalton nodded at Danburn when he came to stand with her. "I need for you to be your dragon. I know that you've not done that yet, not with having so much going on. But to have you standing with us during this trial, it might look as if we're not going to give them any kind of quarter when this is done."

"You want me to be the bad guy in all this." He nodded. "I can do this. But what if my dragon is one of those smaller ones? I don't think that would put much fear in anyone."

"Kip said for you to look at her. She can show you what sort of dragon she is." Dalton started to tell Danburn that she was silver, but he continued speaking. "I know about your child, Dalton, so I want to assure you that there will be no harm done to it. You'll all be safe."

"I don't mind. Kip told me that a dragon child was nearly impossible to harm. Something about the way the dragon within me would protect it." Danburn nodded. "All right. I'll do this for you. It'll actually make me feel better if I could stand next to Kip while this is going on. He's afraid of what they'll say. Okay, not afraid, but he isn't going to be happy

128

about things they'll say."

"I don't blame him. I know them well."

She knew that as well, and went with him. As soon as she was able to shift, it took her a few moments to get Trust to want to do it. When Dalton told her who was on trial, she was more than willing to come out.

"You're silver," Danburn said, open mouthed.

I don't think that's bad, is it? Danburn shook his head. *I would have thought that his mother was silver too. Wouldn't she have been?*

"No. Not necessarily. The dragon will be what is necessary when they are with a new host. Your dragon, as a silver one, is very rare to our kind. But being that you have her, it means that your dragon trusts you beyond anything there is. Congratulations, Dalton. You've been chosen to be someone rare and special."

Her dragon was huge too. She knew that the males were usually larger than the females, but Danburn told her that she was more his size, larger than her human side.

She moved to the table just as Steven and Bethany were brought in. Shackles were at their wrists and ankles. There was even one at their throats that kept them together. She hadn't known what to expect when they were brought here, but she knew that it wasn't for them to look so frail and worn down. She asked Kip about that.

"They've been working at the digs for the better part of a month. Not working so much as giving the illusion of working. Danburn thinks, and I agree with him, that they've made themselves look this way to play on the sympathy of the courts. It won't work, however. We have video of them putting dirt and mud on their bodies and practicing how to look like they do now." She called them asses. "Yes, well, when this starts, you'll hear just how much worse they are."

"Mr. Newton, you are—" Steven said that he was Lord Newton. "You are no longer any such thing. All your titles have been taken. Your castle, after extensive clean up, has been donated to the city, and will soon be opened to the public. The grounds have also been made to look better. You are guilty of taking a part of the earth and destroying it, among other things."

"I demand to know where my son is. If we are to be here, then he should be as well. I have many misdeeds that he did as well." He pointed his finger at Kip.

Dalton's dragon asked her to trust her. *I trust you with my very life. You do what you need to and make this end well.* The snort of fire that Trust blew at the two of them missed them by only inches. Dalton laughed when Steven jumped back and pulled down Bethany when he fell. *You are wonderful.*

No one said a word about what she'd done. She could see that Kip was having a hard time hiding his laughter. Danburn seemed to not care, and was laughing hard and loud. Steven spoke again, his voice harder than before.

"What is the meaning of this? You have no right to try and burn us when we have no way of defending ourselves." Danburn told him that if the dragon had wanted to harm them, they'd no longer be standing there. "That is not right and you know it. I demand that you—"

"You make a great many demands when you are in no position to do that. Now, as I was saying, you have been accused of a great many crimes. Today you will hear from just a few of the people that you have harmed." Danburn looked up at her with a wink. "If you interrupt me or anyone speaking again, I'll have my dragon burn you to nothing and go home. I certainly have a great deal of better things to do than to bring you before me once again."

"This is most unfair." Her dragon leaned down as if she

were going to do just what Danburn had told them she'd do. "But I will listen. I will try and keep my mouth closed too, but I will have my say in this."

"If you have anything pertinent to say, then I will hear it. Now, let us begin. You were sentenced to help with the mud slides that were killing a great many people. There was a quota that you were to do, and you fell short of it daily. In that, you are now at the mercy of me." Danburn looked at Kip before speaking again. "We will not be hearing from your son today, as he has said his piece when you were put to work. Today, we'll hear from Queen Kassian her list of damages that you have done to her lands."

It looked as if Bethany was going to say something, but Steven pulled hard on the chain that connected them. If looks could have ended this with both Danburn and Kip dead, then it would have happened then. She didn't speak, and Dalton heard her dragon cursing. That made Dalton laugh again.

Kassian entered the area with thousands of her faeries. She also had with her an army of faerie guards that were tall and well-armed. When they looked as if they were going to kill the two people in irons, she asked them to stand down for a moment. Kassian cleared her throat and looked at her before she began speaking.

"You are a beautiful dragon, Lady Dalton. Even with you standing guard on the council this day, my lands and the trees around us have gained so much magic. The waterways, should you wish to swim in them, will also benefit from what you are." She bowed before her. "I would like for you to visit me soon. My castle could use a bit of the magic that you have brought to this land."

When she turned back to Steven and Bethany, the anger around her had the guard standing at attention again. This time she didn't ask them to stand down, but nodded at the two she was here to talk about. A scroll was handed to her by a larger faerie, and Kassian opened it to read from. It was the most surreal thing Dalton had ever witnessed.

"The lands upon which the castle sat were in ruin. The grasses were all but dead, the trees starved for the magic that kept them healthy. The dirt beneath could no more hold a seed than it could hold water for the grasses that were there." She looked at the two as she continued. "Everywhere you went, there was destruction left in your path. Animals that had been on view, you killed them simply because you could. It would not have been so bad had you not left their bodies for all to see. But you did not even partake from them, eating nothing at all. That is a willful killing. A killing that is against every law in all the animals' books. There are other things you have done as well. Stamping out flowers that were in their first budding. Killing the faeries that were there only to care for you. Waterways that were not even on your lands were killed when you killed all the fishes and other creatures that lived beneath the life giving waters, for no other reason than to kill. If I had my way, sir— Nay, you are beneath calling you anything but what you are, monster. If I were to have my way, monsters, I would have you destroyed by the very thing that was to help you along in your lives. Many families of faeries and brownies alike are without support. Loved ones killed by your breath. You are a monster, and have no rights to be on this land other than to be destroyed as you have done to so many."

Kassian turned to the table where Danburn, Kip, and one other man sat. She bowed before them too, and asked that one of the options that were before them to kill the couple would be her faeries. She said that they had all volunteered to do what was necessary.

"Thank you, my lady. You have given me a great gift in

this." She nodded. "I will keep that in mind when it comes time for us to take care of these...well, these monsters."

"Wait a damned minute here. It sounds as if you've already decided that we're to die. That's not right. You can't condemn a man even before his trial is over. What if we have some redeeming answer for these accusations?" Kip asked if they did. "I'm not speaking to you. What gives you the right to sit up there anyway? You're nothing but a terrible son. You wouldn't even help us when we were down on our luck."

"You mean when you had your tears taken from you for hiring hitmen to kill me? Or is it that you lost the castle because of unpaid dues, murdering the land and hiding from this council, this Board of Dragons?" Kip laughed at them. "I don't know what you expected me to do for you. Perhaps rob a bank? Steal away a dragon for you so that you could drain them as well?"

"Who told you about that? Kenneth? He's a liar too. Where is the little shit? We were told that he was given his freedom. I'd like to know what moron did that." The stream of fire from Trust was closer this time. "Tell that thing to behave or I'll have it put in irons as well. I won't have this done to me when I have done nothing that no other dragon has done in their lifetime."

"Really? Name one dragon that is not related to you that has done one thing that you have." The people, dragons too, waited for an answer to the question that Kip asked. "Can't think of any? Want to know why? Because there are none. And those that have done what you have are dead. Imprisonment isn't an option for you, nor was it for them."

"So, you're just going to let them kill us, are you? What sort of son can do that to his own parents? Kassian called me a monster. Well, that's what you are, Kip. A monster that would destroy his parents because you've got your head stuck up so far in that man's ass that you can't see that he's making you do this." Trust asked again for her to trust her. When she said forever, the dragon laid down so that her head was only inches from Steven. "So you're going to sic your dragon on me? Poorly done, son. Poorly done."

"Have I not told you, Father? This is my mate. Lady Dalton. However, I'm not surprised that you don't recognize the dragon. She is well loved, taken care of, and trusted. This is my mother's dragon." Steven's face paled at the words that left Kip's mouth. "We are going to give your dragons to a deserving person too when this is done. Because no matter what spills from your mouth about how you were never guilty of any of the misdeeds that you did, I see no hope of you ever proving it."

"You can't do that. I need them." Kip only smiled. "What does that mean? You plan to have this dragon, your own mother's dragon, kill us? I'm ashamed of you. I no longer wish to be called your father, nor you my son."

"Good, that's fine with me." Dalton had a feeling that Steven hadn't expected that. But Kip not only agreed to what his father said, but also did so quickly, as if he had no trouble with it. "Now, back to your misdeeds. I would call it a much stronger word, but then I'm only second in charge, not first. That is the only reason that you are getting this trial too, by the way. I would have killed you flat out the first time you fucked up."

Trust didn't move back but kept close to the other two, as if she were reminding them that she was there. Her hot breath was scorching their clothing, as well as shining up the irons that they were wearing. It took Dalton a few minutes to realize that it wasn't shining it up, but heating it to red hot.

Others came forward to talk about what the elder Newtons had done to them. She was only half listening, watching the two in front of her. They acted like this was just something that they did every day. That coming to stand before the council was simply that—someone was talking to them and there would be no consequences. She told Kip.

I can see that. I do believe you are correct in what you're saying too. They think just because of me being here, that I'll somehow save them because I did Kenneth. Also, did you notice that no one is mentioning anything that he did? It's almost as if the people testifying against them have come to the realization that Kenneth was never a part of what they did. I find that to be very telling.

She'd not noticed. Dalton had been more focused on the movements of Steven and Bethany than what was being said. Now that she did listen, Dalton noticed something else. His mother was mentioned a great deal too, even though everyone knew that she'd taken her own life. It was just as Kip had said about Kenneth—he wasn't mentioned at all.

"Is there anyone else that wishes to bring evidence against these two?" Her tail smacked hard against the earth, as if to say that Trust had something to say. Danburn must have understood the motion. "Trust, I believe you're called. What do you have to say now? You tell myself or Kip, and we'll translate word for word. This I promise you."

Chapter 10

Trust had already decided that she was going to change her name when this trial was over. She had dug through the memories of her human, and found two that she very much enjoyed. Trust had a feeling that she was going to use one of the names for her own child, and she wasn't going to take that from her. Trust so loved the name Violet.

When she stood up, her body as big as she could make it, she looked down at the two people that she hated more than anything in this world. Now that Felicia was dead, that statement was as true as it could be. Reaching out to Lord Kip, she took a long, deep breath and let it out easily, making sure that she didn't do what she had wanted for so many decades — kill them both.

"When I was nothing more than a hatchling and attached to the lady of the house, she abused my tears from the start. Like purchasing things only to destroy them, because she wanted no one else to have them. Or she would use my tears to buy favors from humans. To harm or kill the younger child, Lord Kipling. Several times while he was in his egg, she went to crush it, using a hammer and my strength to do this deed."

Lord Kip was doing just as he'd said he would, and repeated everything she said as if she were saying it. "It was only my magic, the magic that I gave to him when he was nothing more than a speck of a babe in her womb, that kept him safe. After he was hatched, it became apparent that they were going to murder him somehow."

"What other methods did they use to try and kill Lord Kip?" She told Lord Danburn what she knew and felt, her firsthand knowledge of what she had experienced. "Felicia threw herself down the stairs? And even had her mate burn her belly badly enough to make her ill? That is grounds for ending their lives right there. What else is there, Lady Trust? I would hear as much as you can tell me."

"When the child lived over and over despite their attempts to kill him, they resorted to hiring people to do so when he was older. Men without qualms about killing a child, much less a dragon, when there were so very few of them left." Danburn agreed. It was then that she noticed that all eyes were on her, even though her words were coming from Lord Kip. "Several times over his life I have spoken to my son, Lord Kip's dragon, to save the boy at all costs. Even if he had to take him away from the home that they all lived in. But it did little good. They were still out to get him, and my son was so afraid for his life as well."

"You said that they all were in on this, did you not?" Trust nodded her large head at Lord Kip. "Was Kenneth a part of the scheme to kill me? There won't be any harm done to him. He is free of all things that he did in his past."

"Once. It was only to hold the egg in which the child was growing. He told his sister, Bethany, that he would do no more to the child. It made him ill to think of a small being to be crushed under her hammer." People murmured at such a thing, but she was telling all now and paid no attention to

138

what was going on around her. "Iron was crushed up and put into his food by his mother. The father, no better, tried to sell him to a group of men that would tear him apart to sell off his body in parts. It was hard for us to care for him when we, ourselves, were being abused. My mate, the dragon yonder, was abused even when he was out as a dragon, burning down homes and banks so that they might rob them. Then when they were unsuccessful, they would order him to the ground to stay there while the others, in their other forms, would beat him until he could barely fly or live."

"Trust."

She turned in time to see a group of armed men coming at her. Men dressed as if they had thought to buy things that would shield themselves from a dragon. She blew fire at them, melting their armor to their bodies. The iron in their hands burnt through them. Trust knew who had hired them — Bethany and her father, to kill the people that had sent them here. As she drew in breath to kill Steven and Bethany, Danburn, king of all dragons, stood up.

"Halt." She wanted so badly to kill them. To destroy them like they were no more than the scum that they were. Lord Danburn stood before her and put his hand on her chest plate. "You have every right to want them dead. I do as well. But there is an order to things. Rules that must be followed. You know them as well as I do."

Yes, but they do not apply to monsters. He agreed with her, but said that they must do this correctly. It took her long moments to quell her anger. Trust had never been in a position that she could have killed them. But she knew that she must lay her hopes in the king. Bowing before him, she spoke again through Lord Kip. "I shall await your answer, my lord. I do not have to be happy about it, but I will wait."

After thanking her, he went back to his table. The three

men spoke quietly, and it was then that Dalton spoke to her. If nothing else in the world ever turned out correctly, she knew that having Dalton with her was the best this world could have offered her.

You are all right? She said that she was angry. *Yes, well, I can feel that. You sure do get hot when you're pissed off, don't you?*

I do. Have I injured you? Dalton laughed and Trust felt better. *I should like very much to be called Violet after this is done. It is much better and a softer name. I have seen the name in your head.*

It's a flower. The violet is a beautiful flower that is in as many colors as you can imagine. Sort of like you when the sun hits you. That's a beautiful choice, Violet. I will show the flower to you when spring comes again. Violet thanked her, loving the sound of her name being voiced by her new human. *I'm so glad that we could work together. It's nice having a friend that also can take out an army of men.*

They were still talking when Danburn and the others seemed to have come to a decision. Dalton knew that Steven and Bethany were going to die, and die today. Just how they died was going to be up to them.

"Unusual, but we have three ways for you to die." Steven asked why he'd not gotten to speak on his behalf. "Because everything that spilled from your mouth would be a lie. Not only that, but I, for one, am sick of you being right here and breathing. I want you dead more than anything that I've ever wanted. As a man with a mate and child, I would have thought that impossible to beat. As I was saying, we have three ways for you to have your lives ended."

"You're not going to kill me. I had nothing to do with anything. I mean, if you're going to believe a fucking dragon over me, then there is something seriously wrong with you." Bethany lurched forward, dragging her father with her. "I demand my own trial. Where that fucking dragon isn't here to tell lies on me. I never harmed by brother. We were the best of buds growing up. Tell them, Kip. Tell them so that I can have my freedom like you did for Kenneth."

"No."

Kip said no more, and Violet was impressed with him. Here was a man of worth. A man with strength. Not just of mind, but his body as well. Violet bowed before him when he addressed his family once again.

"When this day is over, I will think of you never again. I will not shed a tear for your loss, nor will I tell my children of you. Oh, before I forget, we're to have a baby, Dalton and I. And as of Christmas day, we have adopted four more children that would have been your grandchildren and your nieces and nephews. Too bad for you that you'll never see them grown. You'll never hear them call you Grandda nor Aunt. It is your fault that you are here. My family, my wife and children, will, after this day, never think of you again."

Danburn stood up then, his humor apparent on his face. It did take him several moments to control his laughter to say what he had to say. Repeating that there were three ways they could die, he finally was able to name them.

"You can be killed by fire. Dalton and Kips' dragons will do that for you. You can die by faerie. That will be done to you here, upon this field. With both the earth will be blackened by your deaths, but I have vowed that I will make it healthy again. The third thing that you can die by is imprisonment. You will be put into an iron cell with iron on your arms and legs. It will be a long and suffering death. Really, that's the one that I hope you take. You have five minutes to choose, or I shall."

"Five minutes? That isn't nearly enough time. I would demand that you change it to a year. This is going to be a big undertaking for us." Danburn said no. "I will report you, young man. See if I don't. Five minutes to—"

"You only have three left."

Bethany started to protest but Steven pulled on her chain again. That started a fight between them.

It was comical, really, to watch them fight with each other in this form. She had been the one that had taken so much abuse from them over the years, and having them fight like they were, tossing blame at themselves, did her heart good, thought Violet.

"Time." They were both covered in mud, their clothing torn more too. And the dirt in their hair made it stand up nearly straight, giving them the appearance of being quite mad. "Which will it be?"

"Dragon," shouted Steven. Bethany opted for faerie. Turning his back on them, they were separated, their chains not removed except the ones that tied them together. As an army of faeries seemed to ready themselves, Kip shifted to his dragon. It occurred to her why Steven looked so happy. He thought he was still a dragon. Violet asked Danburn about that.

Thank you, my lady, I forgot to mention that. Putting up his hand, the people were quieted. She drew in a deep breath when Lord Kip did. It was time, and the sooner they were ready, the sooner this would end. "I did forget to mention that you no longer have your dragons. They were taken from you the moment that you were brought before me. You are now and forever, at least for the next few minutes, humans. Goodbye."

The fire spilled from her mouth as did it from Lord Kip's. It burned the man standing there, his screams more satisfying than she'd thought they would be. As he fell to the ground, his body in a full armor of flames, Violet laid down next to

Lord Kip and waited for the rest of the sentencing. Then she looked over at Bethany.

She was acting as if it mattered little to her that her father was now dead. She wondered if Bethany still believed that she might be saved from death. When the faeries came to sit upon the two of them, both her and Lord Kip, she felt their magic healing her from the usage of her flames.

It didn't hurt her to use them. It was only that it depleted her body somewhat. Violet could have gone for a long time, using her flames as necessary. It wouldn't replenish until a group of faeries came to her aid. She watched as she healed to see what was to become of Bethany.

"Now that he is gone, you can allow me to go on my way. He was the one forever telling me what to do. You'd not believe what sort of things that he would do to me when I refused to do what he made me." Danburn just crossed his arms over his chest. "You're going to allow me to be freed, aren't you? I mean, I only said the faeries could do the deed to make it look to Father like that was what was going to happen. I'm not a bad person, Danburn. Just a woman that was...well, I was misled. By my parents. You cannot make me suffer for them. It wouldn't be fair."

"I tell you what, Bethany. If you can name one thing, a single act of kindness on your part, I will allow you to go free. It will have to be the truth or you will receive your punishment right away." She nodded, and Violet wondered what he was doing. She would be set free? "It will be the truth, as I said, or all deals are off."

Bethany stood there for several minutes, thinking. The buzzing of the wings of the readied faeries sounding like music, countdown music that she'd heard on television shows. Danburn told her again that it only had to be one and she would be free. Smiling finally, Bethany looked at him.

143

"I was never successful in killing Kipling." No one moved, the entire group of people stunned, as Violet was, into silence. The faeries, their wings still humming, were no longer chattering to each other, but waited on Lord Danburn.

"Kill her."

~*~

Kip walked through the house that they'd filled with things from their shopping trip. He noticed that there were other things too that had been added. Some of the faeries had made small frames to hold the pictures of themselves. There were larger ones of him and Dalton. When she came into the room with him, Dalton sat down on the couch with a baby in each arm. Sitting down beside her, he took April and handed her the cup of juice and a snack that her faerie brought for her. Dalton did the same for May when she was handed the same kind of food.

"April and May Newton. I guess they're Lady April and Lady May now, aren't they?" Dalton just nodded. "You're upset. I know that, because you usually talk to the girls, and you've not said a word to them in two minutes. What is it, love?"

"I keep thinking about the way the faeries killed Bethany. I mean, it's nothing less than she deserved, but it was brutal, don't you think?" He said that was why they were so good as an army for the queen. "Perhaps, but I have a feeling that they made her suffer longer than they should have. Again, it was nothing less than she deserved, but I can't help but think that they did that for us."

"They did." Kip and Dalton looked at Button when she spoke, bringing a flower for each of the little girls. "The other children have faeries now. It was a hard thing, picking them for the boys. They seemed to think that it was a little girl thing to have and not for them."

144

"How did you convince them that they needed them?" She didn't answer him, but played with April while she drank her juice. "Button, what did you do?"

"I did nothing, my lord. But Peek and Boo—those are their names, I swear it—showed them some of the magic that they had for them. The clothing that you purchased for them is nice, I was told, but these are the things that they really wanted. I'm not sure I approve of them, but they are happy, and that is all I care about." Dalton asked about the killing of Bethany. "They had been injured, my lady. Badly at times, by the entire family, with the exception of Lord Kip. The ones that were there that day, the faeries, they were the ones that had lost loved ones at the hands of the former lord and lady. The Newton's took children too, if you wish to know that. Oh, how they made them suffer. But as for how they killed Bethany—the faeries drove their small bodies through Bethany then healed her as they exited. Not fully, mind you, but enough that her suffering was as great as theirs had been. It was...how should I say? It was what the faeries needed for them to have closure."

The girls were put on the floor when they seemed to be finished. Their faeries were called Blue and Max. They were trying to teach the girls to walk to them. It was funny really, Kip thought. The children, even as young as they were, would crush them should they fall. But too, they seemed to know that they shouldn't hurt the little flying bugs. And the laughter coming from them all was better than any music he'd ever heard.

Brody and Ryan came downstairs an hour later, and Kip thought that the clothing that they had on was very nice. He could see where Button didn't approve of it. The colors were dull, nothing like the flowers that she visited each day. Brody had Peek on his shoulder, and Boo was in Ryan's hands as they came into the room with the girls.

"I was wondering if we could see your dragon." Kip nearly said yes, but Dalton stopped him. She asked about their rooms, if they had cleaned them up or not. Brody smiled. "We have so much, Dalton. I mean, like a hundred million more things than we ever had before. I like to lay them out and look at them when I can. I'm not afraid that you'll take them away, but it is nice having a pair of shoes that fits me, and a coat for all seasons. I've never in my life had a raincoat before."

"So, your clothing is all over the room?" Brody laughed. It, too, was a sound that he loved. "Should I check?"

"No, ma'am. I hung them up. But I do take them out and look at them. I love my tennis shoes, and if you'd not told me, I would never have worn them because they're so white and new." She told him that she was sorry. "I'm not. It's made me appreciate the things that you've given me. And not just clothing and such, but a room of my own. A bathroom that I don't have to share with ten or more other people. I have food whenever I want it. Hot food, too. You've given Ryan and me, and the babies, something that we never dreamed of having. Parents that will be there for us when we need someone."

"My mom and dad, they died from drugs. When I was found at the house with their bodies, I was thinking of ending my life with them. I was starving and cold. There wasn't heat or blankets in the house. I used them to put over their bodies when they started to smell." Kip asked Ryan why he didn't call someone sooner. "They told me, my parents, that the cops were never to be trusted, and if I ended up in the system, I might as well be dead, that's how much they cared for kids like me. But that night, I figured dead was dead, and I was too hungry to care how it happened."

"I'm sorry, both of you. What you endured was horrific, and I wish I could have found you sooner." Brody nodded and Ryan dropped his head. Kip said his name softly to have him look at him. "I am sorry, Ryan. No child should have to go through what the two of you did."

"Are you going to make me go back?" Kip was startled by the question, but did ask him why he thought that. "I was gonna kill myself. I know that's not right. But you have to know, Kip, I was very scared. I'll tell you right now, it was scarier living there with them dead and all than it was to play that stupid game where they throw the big ball at you like it's a cannon."

Kip hugged them both. They didn't much care for being touched, but they were getting used to the hugs that he and Dalton gave them. Two weeks they'd been living with them, and things, he thought, were getting better for them all.

One night a week they went to get dinner. Kip had been surprised that they didn't want pizza every time. They'd done it twice now, and they'd had burgers one night out, and the second week they'd wanted to go to the movies and eat popcorn. He was fine with that, but they did have to eat a meal first. That night they had subs from the local joint. Tonight he was wondering what they wanted to devour, because that was how they ate.

They didn't go at their food like animals, they were polite and well-mannered about it. But they ate like they would never get another meal. Kip supposed that that habit would break soon, as they were happy to have a meal every night.

"I was thinking that we'd like to go somewhere with something besides paper plates." Kip asked Brody what he meant. "Well, I know that you have money, and we'd never ask for something like this if we really didn't want to try it. But we both been doing some research on the place, and it sounds like a place we can enjoy. I read the reviews, and it's got a lot of stars for being so good. Out of six thousand reviews it still had five stars."

"What's the name of the place? This is a school night, and you can't be up too late if we have to drive far to get there and back." Brody assured him that it was close, and told him the name of the place. "Dragon's Lair, huh? Well, why not? Just so you both know, if you don't eat all your dinner, the cook comes out and beats you to a pulp. Also, by the same token, if you love it, she comes out of the kitchen and gives you hugs and kisses."

"I don't know then. Both of them sound like a bad deal to me." Both he and Dalton laughed at Ryan when he made a gagging sound. "I don't mind hugging you and the aunts, but a cook? Does she have big burly arms and hugs with your face in her giant boobies?"

"It's your Aunt Quinn." Both boys asked if he was serious. "Yes. She's been running it and cooking there for a while now. And you're right about the stars. No one goes away from there hungry. She's good. You have to save room for pie, though. It's like biting into a piece of heaven, I swear it."

"Well, let's go then. I'm hungry." Brody pointed out to Ryan that he was forever hungry. "Yeah, but I'm a growing boy. You are too. And if I'd known that Aunt Quinn was the one cooking, I might have asked to go sooner. You think that she'll give us a discount because we're her favorite nephews?" They were going up to their rooms, and their voices carried down to them.

Kip looked at Dalton. "She might not ever keep them away once she tells them that the meals are on the house. We don't want her to go out of business because two growing boys might bankrupt her." Dalton gathered up the girls to get them ready to go out. She told him that if she did, it would be his fault as he had told them they could go. Laughing, Kip went up with her to the nursery to help with the children.

In just two short weeks, she was becoming a pro at being a mom to all four of the kids. Dalton could change a diaper faster than he could, plus she knew a great deal more lullabies than he did. Which wasn't surprising. By the time lullabies came around, he was already an adult. Not that his parents would have sang them to him anyway, but Dalton was teaching them to him, and he was having fun messing with the words a bit, just to make the girls laugh.

The meal was amazing as usual. He had the fried chicken and the boys both had smothered sandwiches. He'd never heard of that until Quinn had started cooking, but it too was one of his favorites. The girls shared a plate of mashed potatoes and green beans. Mostly they just smashed it into their faces and laughed. There was also a plate of fruit for them, as well as pudding for dessert. He and the boys all had pie, and Dalton had ice cream.

"We need an ice cream shop." He agreed and told her how Carmine had been asking for one for months now. "Well, that should be a high on the job list. I love ice cream."

"But that's vanilla, Dalton. How can you eat plain ice cream when there are so many flavors on the list?" She told Ryan that she liked her ice cream like she liked her cheesecake. "A cake made of cheese? Yuck. I'd rather eat spinach."

Of course that meant that they had to order two slices of cheesecake to assure the boys that it wasn't *yuck* at all. It went over as well as their whole dinner. Delicious and amazing, they told Quinn when she came for her hugs.

They were home before their bedtime. After getting baths and jammies on, the kids were all in bed. Kip went to check on them one at a time, and was surprised to find Ryan awake. He asked if he could talk to him.

"Sure. Don't ever think that you can't, all right? If my door is closed, however, it means I'm working. Okay?" Ryan nodded. "What is it you want to talk about? Girls? I know a lot —"

"Double yuck. No, that's just gross." Kip laughed. "I wanted to know if I saved up my money, could I play football at school. I don't know how much it costs, but they told us at the home it was too much for them. If you don't want to, then that's all right too."

"I'd love for you to play football. I won't take your money for it either. Just last year Uncle Danburn payed for all new uniforms for them. I think you'd love it." Ryan said that would be great. "You remind me when sign-ups are on, and we'll get you registered. Is that okay with you?"

"Yes, that's perfect. I have wanted to play football my entire life. Football is my life, Dad."

Ryan rolled to his side and told him goodnight. Kip was still stuck on the dad word. Leaving the room, he leaned against the wall. It was that or fall. He was a dad.

Chapter 11

Making love to Dalton was like a marathon race to him. It was fast fast fast, then they would lay in each other arms sated. Tonight, however, he wanted to move slowly, to give her everything he had. It had been a good couple of weeks, and he wanted his wife badly.

Taking her breast into his mouth, he suckled on it softly, trying his best not to be rushed as Dalton was trying to do. Lifting his head up, he stared at her and could see her passion, her need, and it made his cock ache to finish. But Kip was determined to take her slowly, even if it nearly killed him to do so.

"You're beautiful." She begged him to hurry. "Not this time. I want to memorize every part of your body. I need to make sure that everyone knows that you belong to me."

"It will be all you have once you are dead. Because as much as I love that you're a romantic right now, I can't help but feel like you're going slowly to make me suffer. Just so you know, I will make you suffer in ways that you'll feel for the rest of your— Christ, yes, that's it."

Kip watched her face as he filled her over and over,

pounding into her until he was sure that she could feel him all over her body. Each time he pulled from her heat slowly, savoring each muscle as it tightened around him. The way her hot breath heated his own skin when she inhaled sharply.

Pulling her bottom closer to him, he held onto her tightly as he took her as quickly as she wanted, and slow enough that he could watch her face as Dalton begged him for more. He'd give it to her, he promised her, but in his own good time. She wasn't having any of it, he thought, when she dug her nails into his back and cried out his name when he bit down on her tender shoulder.

Never had a woman made him feel like such a man. Made him think that he could conquer it all. Kip thought that he could take on the biggest bad guy. He could fill the world with riches. All the while, he'd keep her safe for him while loving her with all his heart.

"Come for me, Kip. Please. I want your cum." He told her in good time. "You'd better be thinking that right now is a good time, or so help me, I'll rip you apart."

"Such violence. Whatever has come over you to threaten me so meanly?" She laughed, then cried out when he moved into her deeper. "That's it, Dalton, come for me so that I can take you to wonderous heights."

He would build her up before letting her come just a little. He'd not have known it was possible to do this with a woman if he'd not met her. Dalton loved sex, and she loved it with a small bit of teasing. But once he went too far, she would also let him know that.

"I love you, Kip. Forevermore." He held her to him, telling her that he loved her as well. "We should have lots of babies. Lots of dragons that we can raise to be just like you. A good man."

"What about our daughters? Don't you want to have

152

another daughter or two that will be just like you?" She laughed and moaned at the same time, then asked him if he could handle any more like her. "I will, because I will love them as much as I do you."

He took her harder then, feeling that she was getting frustrated more and more. One thing he didn't want to happen right now was for her to stab him in the back. She would—Dalton had been pissy like that before.

Bringing her to her peak once more before he made her scream was something that he'd gotten good at too. And when she bent back, her body nearly in half with her release, Kip took her breast into his mouth and bit down hard enough to taste her blood.

It was there, the taste of the hormones that made the child that she was carrying. The taste of her blood was richer. Her skin was covered in the dewiness of her being with child. When Kip came, crying out from the pain and pleasure of it, he held her to him as he came twice more.

Holding her in his arms, both of them breathing hard, he had a small chuckle at the thought that came to him. When she asked him what was so funny, her breathlessness making him laugh harder, Dalton curled her fingers into his hair and pulled his head up to see her face.

"You are the most beautiful creature that I've never seen. I will love you forever and a day, Dalton Newton. And when we are old and our children are settled around us, I will tell you once again just how very much it means to me to have had children like us."

They slept well that night. He supposed he had worn them both out. When he woke, there was a note in the bathroom from Dalton, telling him that she had to go into town earlier than usual, so he dressed to go to work too. He didn't really have to work—neither of them did. It was nice to have a place to go that would mean that he was doing something and not being bored.

Going to the kitchen, both Brody and Ryan were in there having pancakes, and the girls, both dressed, were having what looked to him like mushy food. It turned out to be pancakes too, but little girl style. He kissed them on the heads and hugged the boys. Today was Friday, and they had plans with them all for the weekend.

"I have done up their lunches, my lord. There is a meeting this morning at school for Brody." Kip glanced at Brody, who then shoved away his plate and dropped his head and shoulders. "Ryan has a list of things that he needs for his classes too. The list is here on the refrigerator." He pulled it off and asked Ryan when he needed it. After telling him Monday, he knew that he'd get it today so it wouldn't mess with their weekend.

Kassian had invited them all to her castle to have a look at the animals. Martha asked if they needed anything for tomorrow. Martha said that she'd make something if they needed it.

"We're only to bring ourselves, I was told." Martha nodded and said that she could handle that. "Should we bring anything like a gift?"

"I'd not, sir. I think the children being there will be enough for her." He nodded and gathered the boys up to drop them off at school. "I'll watch over the wee ones, sir. There is plenty of help around to keep them happy."

He had his meeting set up for while he was there. Kip hadn't talked to Brody about the meeting. He seemed upset enough as it was. Even getting out of the car, he didn't seem like the boy he'd been just last night. Whatever was going on, he'd get to the bottom of it.

This school was progressive, and he liked that the boys

seemed to be happy there. At least Ryan did. Brody's teacher and the principle showed up about the time that Dalton came in. He'd told her if she could, she might want to be there too.

"I've been talking with Brody about several assignments, and he isn't doing them correctly. He's not caught up." The papers were handed to Dalton, and Kip asked the teacher what sort of assignments he was messing up on. "Math, for one thing. He is so far behind that I will have to give him a failing grade on this paper, and more than likely the next two tests too."

Mr. Howard spoke up and asked if she'd worked with him. Her answer was that she had twenty-eight other children that needed her time more. Brody, she told him, was not caught up.

"That's the second time you've said that. That he's not caught up. Are you saying that the young man that you have in your class, my son, is behind? Because that stands to reason, since he'd never been to a classroom like this. He was in an orphanage for most of his life." Dalton handed the papers to him and he only glanced at them. Dalton had this. "Mr. Howard, when we placed the boys in this school, you assured us that they'd have tutors that would help them catch up with the rest of the class. It sounds to me like that's not happening."

"As I said, I have twenty-eight other students that are caught up and working at my pace. I will not have him disrupting the entire class by asking questions all the time." Kip looked at Dalton when she stood up. The teacher, Mrs. Monroe, did as well. "What do you expect me to do, *Lady Dalton?* Cater to his every whim when I have more important, smarter children in my classroom?" Mrs. Monroe sneered her name like it was a curse word.

"I expect you to teach those that have a need for you to,

you fat cow." Mrs. Monroe looked at Mr. Howard. He didn't say a word, but did cover his mouth. "What you will do is stop making my son feel bad about himself and his being behind, and help him."

"I am only pointing out to the other children that he is the one keeping us from going to the next chapter. I guess I'm lucky now that he didn't learn a habit from you by calling his teacher names." Mr. Howard asked her if she'd really said that to the other children. "Of course I did. I want them to know who is sucking up all the time we have. Have you any idea how many questions he can ask in an hour's time? I won't have it. He's disruptive by not being on the same level as the other children. He should be put back where he came from. They're worthless, system sucking kids, and they'll grow up as the same thing."

"That's enough. Sit down." Mrs. Monroe sat down, and when she started to stand up again, Kip only had to look at her. Kip looked at Mr. Howard. "Is this the kind of teachers that you have here? You allow them to humiliate children that didn't have the benefit of being as caught up as the others? I have no doubt whatsoever that she is telling them this, as well that my son is a welfare child."

"I do. Why shouldn't they be aware of the kind of things we have in the classroom?"

Dalton drew back her fist and hit the woman right in the face. Kip was sure that he should have stopped her, but he didn't want to. Instead, he called out to Danburn and Kendrick.

I need you at the middle school now, if you please. I might change that to jail before this is over. Kendrick asked what had happen, her laughter coming through loud and clear. *My son Brody is being humiliated and targeted by his math teacher. Dalton just hit her and knocked her out. Please hurry.*

156

Her tone changed when she answered him. *I'm nearly there now. Danburn, you come too. You might have to bail all of us out if they're doing shit like this to my nephew.* Danburn said that he was closer, but she'd better hurry if she wanted a piece of this. *You don't let me have my fun and I'll hurt you.*

An ambulance was called. Kendrick did beat Danburn there, but only by seconds. By the time the ambulance had arrived, Mrs. Monroe was awake and screaming her head off. Kip didn't even mind that they were headed to jail. They were lucky that Dalton hadn't killed the woman.

~*~

"I'm so sorry, Lady Kendrick. I swear to you I had no idea this was going on." Kendrick had told them to talk to her. Dalton was still angry, and getting madder by the moment when Brody was called to the office to verify what was being said about him. Daily. Mr. Howard looked at her. "Lady Dalton, when Mrs. Monroe wanted this meeting, I thought it was to have some help from home for the young man. I've spoken to him and his brother several times in the hall, and neither of them mentioned this was going on."

"She bullied them." Mr. Howard nodded at Dalton when she spoke, her voice full of anger. His head looked as if it might be in danger of falling off. "This family, all of us, have donated a great deal of time and money to this school to have kids have a good start on college. Now I hear that not only are you humiliating them in front of the entire school, but you're targeting them because they might need just a little more help than others. That is not what we wanted when we decided to have my sons come here."

"Mr. Howard, where is the tutor that was promised to Lady Dalton for her boys? I know for a fact that you told them that there would be help to catch them up. Where did that fall through the cracks?" Kendrick winked at her as she continued. "I'm not so sure I'd want my children going here anymore. I mean, as it stands right now, I don't even want to help the school when you have needs."

"Oh no, please, my ladies. I had no idea this was going on. I assure you that I will take care of this right now." Dalton told Mr. Howard that wasn't soon enough. "I had no idea."

"If you say that to me one more time I'm going to hurt you." He nodded and snapped his mouth closed. "You should have known it. I saw in the brochure that you personally monitor the classes once a month to make sure that the children are getting the best of educations. What happened there? And don't you dare tell me that you didn't know. You had to know, you dick head."

Kendrick laughed and stood up when Lady Elissa came into the room. With a snap of her fingers, not only did Mr. Howard leave, but Mrs. Monroe—who had refused to go to the hospital as she had twenty-eight children to teach—was sitting in his place.

"You're fired. You'll be very lucky if I don't take away your pension and your other teacher perks. Now tell me again why my grandson is being treated like he's beneath you. Because as it stands right now, he could buy and sell this entire school several times over without batting an eye." Elissa sat down finally, but was not finished. "You will not work again, in this district or any other, for as long as I live. And let me tell you, that is a great deal longer than you will live. I cannot fathom why you would do such a thing to an eager young man. He didn't deserve this at all."

"You can't fire me. I don't know who you think you are, but you have no authority to fire me." Danburn came into the room and Mrs. Monroe didn't bat an eye as she continued. "You can't either. Just because you have money to throw around on anything you wish, that does not put you in a position to fire anyone. I'll appeal it even if you do. I belong to the teachers union, and they'll have my back."

Danburn laughed, and Dalton wanted to hit him too. Instead she waited with the rest of them while not only was Danburn found a chair, but Brody was brought to them. Another man, a stranger, came into the room as well. There were too many in such a small room.

"Brody, I want you to tell me what your math teacher said to you daily. No one here is upset with you. Just tell me." When Danburn spoke Brody looked at her, and she smiled and told him to go ahead. "I promise you, son, nothing will happen to you."

"She said that I was stupid, and then she had the other teachers think that too. My spelling teacher makes me sit in the hallway because she said that I have head lice. I don't, Uncle Danburn. I don't." Danburn said that he believed him. Dalton stared at the woman who'd caused all this. "I'm not allowed to eat with Ryan, either. I have to sit all by myself at one table, and he sits at the other table. Nobody wants to play with us because she told lies about us."

"Why didn't you tell anyone?" Brody looked down at his feet and Dalton wanted to get up and hug him to her. This was so wrong on so many levels. "Why didn't either of you tell someone? You know that we would have done something about it before now."

"She said that she'd hurt me." That was all she could take and she stood up. Her dragon moved along her skin, and Dalton so wanted to let her go. But a word, one she didn't understand, had her dragon curling around her. Danburn had stopped whatever she had wanted to do to the woman. But she did take her son into her arms.

Brody cried and told her how sorry he was. She was so worked up that she could only tell him that she loved him.

Dalton did love him, all the kids she now got to call family. Dalton looked at Danburn.

"This has to be taken care of, Danburn. Who knows how many other children she has treated this way?" He said that he was taking care of it. "I don't want it taken care of. I want it ended. With her being unable to talk to children like that again."

"Trust me, Lady Dalton, I will take care of it." The stranger spoke for the first time. Then he lifted up the small device that she just noticed on his leg. "Have you heard enough, board members? Do you think this is the time to do what we talked about earlier when I came here?"

There were several "ayes" said to the man. Then he thanked them—the board, Dalton assumed—and stood up. Mr. Howard was called into the room then, and the man said to call all the teachers to the gymnasium. He was going to talk to them.

"What's going on?" Mr. Howard was told to do as he was told and he left them. Another phone call was made, and the police came in and arrested Mrs. Monroe.

"There will be others, I'm sure, so you should send over more officers, please." The man finally introduced himself to everyone in the room. "My name is Jonas James. I am the president of the teachers' association. We're taking action right now, Lady Dalton. Had I known that this was going on, this would have been taken care of before your sons were subjected to such horrid words against them."

Brody was asked to give a list of the teachers that had mistreated him. Ryan was asked to talk about his trouble too. Ryan was much more lighthearted about things, but Dalton could tell that it was hard for him. In the end he was crying too, and showed them the bruise that he'd gotten from Mrs. Tayler, the art teacher.

As they were asked to wait for the meeting too, she held the boys and talked to Kip. She was distraught about all this. Dalton felt like the worst parent in the world. Her sons were hurt, physically too, and she'd not known. She told Kip just what she was feeling, but it was Brody that spoke first.

"How do you think you're the worst kind of mom? Geez, Mom, nobody in my life ever stood up to someone for me." Brody looked at Ryan before he continued. "I guess you were right, Ryan. I should have told them when I was getting slammed like that. But there isn't any reason for you to think that you did us wrong. It was our fault. We should have trusted that you'd take care of us when you said that you would."

"You called me Mom." Brody grinned. "I've never been called that before. I love it. And I love the two of you. I do hope, however, that in the future you trust us to have your back in this."

"Ryan, you should have seen Mrs. Monroe's face. It was all swollen and puffy, like she'd been fighting like those guys on the television. Geez, I wish I could have seen Mom hit her." Kip said that it wasn't right to hit someone. "I know, you're right. But I still wish I could have seen it."

"It was epic." Dalton told Kip that he wasn't helping. "What? I just wanted them to know that their mom has a nice left hook. And it only took her one hit to knock the woman flat on her ass."

"Kipling Aaron Newton, what are you teaching my grandchildren?" He was smiling when Elissa walked into the room speaking. She looked at the boys before speaking. "If I hear that you use violence to get your point made, I will be very disappointed in you both. I have to tell you, however, I'm very proud of your mother. She's taken being your mom to the next level, and it's only been two weeks. What do you think she's going to do for you when you're older? I'm betting people will fear her. I do at times."

The meeting was about to get underway when they joined the teachers and Mr. James in the big room. Brody sat close to her, and Ryan next to his father. The teachers on Mr. James's list, including two that hadn't been named, were asked to come forward.

"You're all fired." They looked shocked, but the police escorted them out of the room. Apparently, their personal things had been packed up for them, and they were to leave any keys they had too. "Now, I would like to talk to the rest of you. As of this day we will be closing down the school for two weeks. You will all suffer, I'm afraid, as I will not be paying any of you for that time."

Grumblings were made, but no one got up to object. It was then that Mr. James talked about what had happened with two of the students that were attending there. He didn't mention their names, but Dalton had a feeling that they knew just who they were. One teacher stood then. Her name was Miss Martin.

"I'm glad that this is happening, sir. I have my resignation all ready to turn into the board on Monday. I cannot work in a place that condones the way that those other teachers were treating those boys. Brody is in my classroom for fifth period. It's science, and I've never had a more curious and wonderful young man in any of my rooms." Two more teachers stood and said that they had the boys in their class and enjoyed them. "I did offer to help them with their math, going as far as asking for his parents' phone number so that I could offer directly to them, when Marylyn, Mrs. Monroe, said that she didn't have it. Stating that more than likely his parents were out spending their fortunes on other undeserving children. I was appalled by that. And going to Mr. Howard did no good whatsoever."

"Did any of the rest of you teachers that had these young men in your classes go to Mr. Howard?" All of them had, and also had their resignations in hand. Mr. James told them all how profoundly sorry he was about that. "We're going to be using this two weeks to find better teachers. Please don't turn those in unless you have made up your mind for sure."

Kip stood up then and asked if he may address the room. Mr. James stepped back and Kip smiled at the teachers. Dalton didn't know what was going on—he and Danburn and Mr. James had spoken for some time before the meeting was called to order. Dalton couldn't imagine what he was going to do now. Whatever it was, she would support him to the ends of earth.

"Hello. Most if not all of you know who I am. For the few that do not, I'm Kipling Newton. The titles aren't important to what I have to say." He winked at her, and she smiled back. "Starting today, at noon, I was appointed as temporary principle of this school."

The cheers were deafening. The teachers were yelling hooray and saying that he should have taken the job years ago. When they were ready to settle down, Kip spoke again. He was very stern in his words this time.

"Temporary doesn't mean that I'm going to slack off in my duties. I will take this position seriously, and do what I need to do make sure that no child suffers as mine and countless others have. There are rules that we will follow. Guidelines that are there for us to use. I want to also say that I do have two sons that go here. I would like to promise you that I won't be keeping an extra eye out for them. But after today, this last couple of weeks, I doubt any of you don't understand why I would." He looked over at her. "My lovely wife, Dalton, has been a cop for a great many years. I'm hoping that we can work out something for keeping the school safe by having safeguards put in place in case of a school shooting. I will also ask for her help in hiring a good group of teachers. They, along with all of you, will have background checks. You'll be fingerprinted. Also, I'll tell you that if you have any keys, to the outside doors or to your rooms, they will no longer work. I am using my own personal money to make sure that no one that has been terminated here will be able to return. It will be done while we're closed."

Danburn stood up then, with Kendrick at his side. They were, Dalton just noticed, a very beautiful couple. Like a wedding cake topper.

"My wife and I will help you along in this change. If you have trouble making ends meet, come to us and we'll see to it that you get help. Also, this is very important too. If you are in need of supplies for your rooms, please give us a list and we'll endeavor to get those to you as well." Kendrick spoke quietly to Danburn, and he turned back to the teachers. "All of you know my wife, so this will come as no surprise to you when I give you her message. She will come here and kick your asses if she ever hears about this happening to any child again. I'd not mess with her if I were you."

Chapter 12

Dalton was still pissed off. Her anger made her stomp around the room as she thought of that woman, what she'd been calling Mrs. Monroe since they arrived home. The only good thing out of this, she thought, was that she had been called Mom. Looking around when Ryan said her name, she bent to his level and kissed him on the forehead.

"We got two weeks off from school." Dalton told him that she knew that, she'd been there. "Brody and I were thinking." The boy laughed so hard that he couldn't finish what he'd been about to say. Brody finished for him.

"What we've been thinking is that we'd like to take a trip." She'd not told them about the one to the Kassian's castle. "That way we can start new when we go back to school. We don't have to go anywhere expensive, just a place we can be together."

"I have a plan for us." She nearly laughed when they looked so crushed. "Do you remember Kassian? She's invited us to her castle. I need to be in her gardens as my dragon, but that won't take long, she told me. I'm going to put a little of my magic there for the flowers and trees to use."

165

"Really? We're going to a real castle?" Dalton nodded. "Holy moly, that will be a blast. What sort of things can we do there? Are her stars different than ours? Do they have different trees than we have here?"

"I haven't any idea. I've never been there either." They were shocked by that, but went to their rooms to make a list of things they wanted to ask the queen. She was still on her knees when Kip joined her in the room. "I told them about the trip. I figured they could use a pick me up as much as I could."

"Good. I was hoping that you'd tell them. I have one more surprise for you." She told him that he gave her too many surprises as it was. "Never. I love watching you glow with happiness. Come here and sit with me. Oh, Martha said that April and May are taking a long nap because they were worn out by the help she had today."

"That reminds me. Do you know why they're called April and May?" Kip told her they were pretty names. "They are, but April was born on the last day of April and May was born four hours later on May the first. Their new birth certificates came today, and I saw that on there. So, what did you get me?"

Kip laughed and handed her a pretty box. It was silvery white and had the most beautiful red bow on the top. Dalton opened it greedily, and couldn't believe what was inside of the pretty little box.

"It's a key." He said that she was right. "I have a house key. But this looks more like a car key. Did you buy a car today?"

"I bought *you* a car today. It has four doors and three row seating. So you can take the boys to school and the girls to daycare." She looked at him to see if he was kidding. "After the uproar that we caused at the school today, Mercy Daycare decided that they'd take the girls in without putting them on a waiting list. I believe they thought you'd come there next and make them. They're afraid of you, my dear."

"Good." She laughed and stood up. Dalton wanted to see her car now. When she saw it, all she could do was squeal in happiness. It was just what she had wanted. A safe, bright silver car that she could drive her children around in. He told her to look inside. "It's a dragon. You got me dragon car seat covers. And look, a decal in the back of a dragon too."

Her dragon was pleased as well. The dragon was well done, and she wondered who had drawn it. Getting into the beautiful car, Dalton could see that someone had gone to a lot of effort to make it special. There were not just dragons around in different places, but faeries too. Even the door locks were small carved faeries that she fell in love with.

She wanted to test drive it, but duty as a mom called. Dalton had hired a tutor for Brody that was coming soon to meet him, and Ryan was going to have one that would help him with his spelling and reading. He didn't enjoy reading at all, and she thought it was because he had trouble making out the words. Her kids were going to be the best. And if they struggled, it would not be from lack of trying.

Dinner was a grand affair for them. Pizzas and Chinese food had been ordered and they shared it all. Brody loved the hot and spicy foods, the hotter the better, just as Kip and Dalton did. Ryan only enjoyed things that didn't burn your taste buds off at the first bite. It was a fun night of discovery and laughter.

When the boys made their way up to their rooms, April and May woke up. It wasn't too late for them to have had a nap. The girls went to bed at eight, and didn't make a sound for the rest of the night. Kip said it was because the faeries in their room kept them entertained until they were sleepy.

She didn't care, it was nice having a good night's sleep all the time.

She and Kip were both reading when someone knocked on the door. Dalton had no idea who would be calling this late, so she went to the door with Kip with her gun out. Dismissing the butler for fear of him being hurt, Dalton waited while Kip slowly opened the door.

"May I help you?" Dalton didn't hear anything from the person on the other side, and that made her a little more jumpy. "My wife has a gun pointed right at your heart. If you don't answer me, then she's going to assume that you're a bad guy and kill you."

"I don't believe you." Dalton fired at the bottom of the door when the man spoke. "I see. So you really have a wife and she really has a gun. Are you always this suspicious?"

"I am. I really am. Now again, what is it you want?" He said money. "So your intent was to come here and rob me? How do you think you're doing so far?"

The door was shoved against her and she fired again, this time aiming at the area where she thought the shoulder was. The man howled in pain, but he didn't push on the door again. Kip opened it the rest of the way and she saw the intruder for the first time.

"I've called the alpha from here. I'd not disbelieve that it's him either, if I were you. Shawn doesn't like to have interruptions to his life as well as my wife does." The man called him a name and Kip laughed. "Yes, well, that's a good one. However, I don't think that's very appropriate, do you? I mean, you don't know me well enough to call me that sort of name, do you?"

"You mother fucker, I'm going to kill you." Kip asked him if he had a death wish. "You must. Why didn't you just go along? Others have."

"Well, we'll have to see that everything that you took from them is returned as well." Kip seemed to be enjoying himself a great deal. And when Shawn simply appeared behind the man, the would be robber screamed. "Do you have him, Shawn? Also, he told us that he's been robbing others around here. I would check him out if I were you."

"I shall. Thank you for bringing this wolf to my attention. I do hope that no one will miss him." With a hard shake, Robber Dude was tossed over Shawn's shoulder. The sound of screams from Robber Dude was cut off when the pack of other wolves made short work of him. "He will never bother you again. I shall take care of the robberies as well. Thank you again, my friend."

Dalton stood there after Kip closed the front door. It was done. She had fired twice at a man, and the pack had come to get him. It was over. Dalton looked at Kip as he began to whistle, walking to the couch where they'd been.

"What just happened here?" He asked her what she meant. "Why did you call Shawn? I mean, why not the police?"

"They would have asked too many questions, and he might not have spent any more time in jail than it would have taken to fill out the paperwork. I thought this way was easier." She asked why he'd called Shawn. "The man was wolf. Couldn't you tell?"

"No. I mean, is there a trick to that?" Kip told her that it was their scent. "I'd like to learn that. I don't want to call on the wrong person when someone comes to rob us."

"I was just thinking about that. You should meet the other leaders in this area. There are a great many of them, so we'll only take you to meet the larger groups." She asked him what he was talking about. "Well, the larger groups around here—vampire, bear, snakes, and tigers." He asked her if she was coming to sit down again.

"You really have vampires around here?" Kip said that she knew one of them. "I think I would remember if I'd met a vampire."

"Mr. Carson at the all night gas station is a vampire. His son is as well." She said no, she'd seen his son out during the day. "He's only part vampire. Mr. Carson's lovely wife is human. Then there is the doctor at the clinic with Cassie. He's a great guy, you should meet him soon."

Her head was spinning as she sat back down on the couch. The murder mystery seemed mundane after finding out about the other groups around here. Dalton asked Kip how many others were there.

"Kassian has a few unicorns on her land. There are other creatures too that people think aren't real. Let me see...there is a griffin there. A few dinosaurs. Those are such beautiful creatures, and the movies have their coloring and bodies all wrong. Anyway, you'll see them all tomorrow." He looked where she had tossed her book. "Did you finish it already?"

"No, I can't read make believe when I'm living it right now." Kip laughed and pulled her into his arms. "Are you kidding me?"

"No, darling, I am not. There are so many creatures that some I do not have a name for there. And here, there are so many that you'd never believe they are what they are." Dalton believed him. She had no idea why, but she did. "Now, let me read this book. I need to know all the rules before we start interviews on Monday morning for the new teachers."

She let him read, but her mind was in turmoil. Not in a bad way, but just overwhelmed, she thought. Dalton lived with a dragon and was one herself, and had trouble believing there were vampires about.

Going to the kitchen, she smiled at Martha when she set a plate of fruit, cheese, and crackers in front of her. Instead of eating them, however, Dalton played with them. She had so many questions on her mind right now that she wasn't sure to begin.

"I'm a tiger, miss." She looked at Martha, who seemed to be as old as stones. "I can show you my real appearance. Not my tiger—she's a little playful and could harm the floors. I mean what I really look like." Dalton asked her why she didn't just be herself all the time. "When I was hired for the job I was told that you knew about shifters, but in your mind you were afraid a wee bit. So, thinking I'd be doing you a big favor by not being me, I searched in your mind as to what you thought a cook should look like. Here I am."

"Change to you, please." In seconds she was a beautiful red head with the most milky complexion she'd ever seen. "I guess you're very old too, aren't you?"

"Yes. Not as old as Shawn, but old." Dalton nodded. "You're stressed out. That's not good for the little ones, nor you. I can have a talk with you should you need it. I was told that you're a very smart and levelheaded young woman."

"You'd think that, wouldn't you?" They both laughed. "Thank you, Martha. Is there anyone else in the house that is hiding their appearance for me? If so, would you tell them to be themselves? I never want to make anyone uncomfortable."

"I can do that, my lady." She put more fruit on the plate when Dalton noticed that she'd eaten it. "You haven't been told as yet, but the baby girls, they're not human either."

She spit her food across the counter and onto Martha. Dalton simply got up and left the kitchen when Martha started laughing harder. Dalton didn't know if she was kidding or not, but she didn't want to know right now. She'd been told they were human, and she was going to stick with that.

~*~

The interviews were going well, Kip thought, and marked

171

the one that he'd just conducted into the no pile. It was larger than the hire pile, but he was all right with that. Cassie had come to help, and she turned out to be a quicker background checker than any police department. When she told him no on the next two, he smiled at the man and conducted the interviews anyway. It was fun for him to see what sort of lies people would tell to get a job.

The next person in line was a hire. Carmine asked to be excused for a moment, and he interviewed Mrs. Hoy as he had the others. There was something about her when he asked her about her past jobs that made him feel dirty. So far today they had had two people come through the lines to be hired that had arrest warrants out with their names for child pornography. The police were there just for that reason.

Uncle Kip, that is not the woman that was next in line with you. Carmine sounded like she was afraid, and that made him frightened too. *She must have cut in line or something. Does she have on a white sweater and a pink blouse?*

No. I see that woman. She's next after this one. I think she did cut in line, and pink blouse woman looks to be pissed. The gun hit the table hard, and he told Carmine to call the police. *Don't come out here. Not at all.*

I can help you and I'm going to. Just don't make any sudden moves. Kip had a thought. A small one, but he wanted things to go perfectly now that everyone was taken care of. *You'll be fine. I'm coming out now. Just ask her what she wants.* He did.

"I need a job, and you're going to give it to me. Or else." He asked her what else what. "You're dead."

The police were leading the other applicants out of the building. Carmine sat down next to him and smiled. The woman seemed very happy about her sitting there and picked up her gun.

"You're just the kind of little kid I like, you know."

Carmine just smiled. "You're just starting to show that you're becoming a woman. Those small titties, and I'm betting that you're starting to have some pretty hair too."

"You won't like me. I'm the kind that can fight back when it comes to people like you." The woman asked Carmine what sort of person she thought she was. "Nasty."

"Nasty?" The laughter coming from her echoed in the room. "Well, you won't think so when I'm finished with you. You'll be—"

Uncle Kip, she's usually medicated and locked up. She escaped this morning from prison after killing one of the guards and taking his gun. There is an all points out on her right now. I've called Aunt Dalton. He asked her why she'd do something like that. *Because she can take care of this without anyone else getting hurt. You have to trust her abilities. If you don't, then all is lost. Tell Mrs. Carson that you know who she is.*

"Mrs. Carson, I know who you are and where you've come from. You should know that the police are here and are going to arrest you." Carmine told him he was doing just fine. To keep talking. "We have a very good background check that we conduct, so we would have weeded you out right away. So why don't you put down that gun and no one will get hurt."

"The only people that will be— How did you know my name? I didn't tell you." He told her that it was on the news. "Oh. I had a problem coming here for the interview. The place where I'm staying, they said that I wasn't fit to come work with children anymore. One little mistake and they banned me for life. Tell me, is that all that fair? No, it's not. I told them I'd behave myself, but they didn't believe me for some reason." She looked over at Carmine again.

"You don't really strike me as a person that could work with children either. You're staring at my niece like she's—

173

well, an apple pie or something." Kip could have kicked himself. What the hell was he saying? But Carmine put her hand on his and he felt himself calm. "You should just give yourself up and go back to where you were staying."

"I don't think they'll let me stay there anymore. I told you, I had a little trouble getting out to come here for my interview. Are you going to do it? I don't know how long I have, but you have to hurry it along now and hire me. That way I can tell them I can't go back because I've found me a good job. It is going to be a good job, isn't it?" It was, he thought, but didn't know what to say to her. Then he saw Dalton. "Answer me."

"Well hello, Mrs. Carson. Do you remember me?" Kip could see the panic in Mrs. Carson's face then. She knew Dalton. Kip was never so glad to see his wife dressed in full body armor as he was right now. "Sir, you and our niece are to get out of here now."

Kip started to stand and the gun went off. He wasn't hurt, he didn't think, but looked at Carmine. She was fine too, she told him, and stood up. He started to stand too, but was stopped when he saw blood pooling in his lap.

It's not as bad as it looks, Uncle Kip. It went into your belly, but it's not hit anything major. You're just losing a lot of blood. He asked Carmine how that constituted as being not bad. *You're not dead, are you?* He wondered what Rette would do if he murdered his daughter. He'd more than likely shoot him where he would be in a lot of trouble.

If he'd not been looking directly at the other two women, he might have missed it. Dalton did a slick move and took the other woman to the floor. As the gun went flying across the room, one of the officers picked it up with a pen and put it into a bag. Other officers, most of whom he didn't have any idea who they were or where they had come from, flooded the room and took care of the woman on the floor.

174

"Are you all right?" He nodded, then shook his head at Dalton. "Yes, well, you look like you've seen a unicorn. I know that they exist now, so you can bet that I know what I'm talking about. The ambulance is here. They're going to take you into the hospital to have the bullet removed. I need it for evidence. Thanks for that."

"Did you just thank me for getting shot?" Dalton grinned and nodded at him. "You're not right in the head, my dear. Not at all."

The woman was screaming about having a job and that she couldn't go back to jail. They all three watched her as she was dragged out the door. Kip thought again how he'd like to have a nice boring day, and said as much to Dalton.

"You'd hate it. Life is boring enough without a little excitement once in a while to get the blood flowing." He showed her his hand covered in his own blood. "Don't be such a baby. You'll be fine. And then we'll go out into the yard and shift, and you'll be as good at new."

"I don't much like you right now." She laughed along with the other cops that were there with him. "Do you always have to have a one liner? I don't feel well — "

When Kip woke, he was not only in a hospital room, but he was in an ugly gown too. Looking for someone to tell him what had happened, he saw Elissa first, reading a book. While he didn't have any idea what she was reading, he knew it was one of her bodice rippers by the cover.

"You know that reading that stuff will rot your brain, don't you?" She looked up at him with a smile. "I don't remember how I got here."

"I'm sure that it'll not be forgotten by the people in the ambulance with you. My goodness, Dalton has a mouth on her." Not sure that he actually wanted to know, he asked her what was said. "She nearly shot one of the men that was helping you. I guess your blood pressure reading was too high. Normal, I guess, for a dragon. Well, he argued with her about it. Then she pulled out her gun and told him she was either going to blow his head off or shift and let him see how high a dragon's pressure was. Of course, she was much more colorful about it. That poor man. I hope he doesn't quit his job over her. I got her to calm down, but I swear, Kipling, his hands were shaking so hard that I didn't think he was going to be able to insert the needle in your arm for the IV that he wanted to start."

"Where is the little hellion now?" Elissa laughed and said that she'd made her go eat. "I love her very much. You know that, don't you?"

"Well of course you do, Kipling. She's the perfect match for you. Oh my, those babies are simply the best thing in the world too. I have to tell you, Brody called me the other day and asked me if I'd like to go to dinner with him and Ryan. I was so shocked, but I told him yes, for him to pick the place. He explained to me that since he'd invited me out, it was my choice on the place to go. Ryan chirped in that you were teaching them manners, and how to ask someone out."

"The two of them have been working odd jobs around the house. They are also helping the faeries to bring in all the things for them to use. Ryan has taken a huge interest in herbs. Anyway, they might insist on paying for dinner. I'd let them. Please?" She asked if they were working that hard. "They're doing well, I think. Dalton has been giving them an allowance too. I've never had that, neither had she, but we sort of winged it. They're happy, I'm happy, and so is Dalton."

She walked into the room as he finished saying her name. After giving him several hugs and kisses, she sat down in the chair that Elissa had been in when she said that she had to go and get some things for dinner. Dalton told him about her day so far, and he asked about the ambulance.

"I don't want to talk about it. I might have gone just a tad overboard on that guy." Kip asked her if she did or she just thought she had. "You scared the fucking shit out of me, if you want the truth of it. You just sort of keeled over. Christ, don't ever do that again."

"I won't, if you promise me that you'll come to my rescue every time I get hurt. Did you really threaten to shoot his head off or eat him as your dragon?" Dalton nodded and he laughed. "I wish I could have been awake for that. That guy must have been green with fear."

"Not as bad as the guy who was driving. I thought he was going to run us off the road a couple of times, he was craning his neck so hard to see what was going on." Dalton laid her head on his shoulder. "I love you, Kip. You can never leave me alone. If you do…. I just don't think that I can survive life without you by my side."

"I won't, love. I promise you. If I do get ill, I'll make sure that I do everything in my power to take you along with me." She nodded. Kip laughed again. "Who would take care of the children if we're both gone?"

"I think that Ryan could do it. He's a goofball, but I swear when there is a crisis, he can be as calming as he is nuts."

She held his hand while she stayed close to him. Watching her blink slower each time, he nearly fell asleep with her. When Danburn came in to see how he was doing, Kip had no problem asking him to come back later. His mate was resting, and he was going to protect her as much as he could. Because after all this, he realized that they needed each other more than most mates did.

Epilogue

Kip loved this time of year. He also loved Christmas, but the summer months, especially July, were his favorite. Everyone, all the families, were able to get together for an entire week, and he more than the rest was so glad to make the extra effort to have his family here all together again.

"You're such a sap." Kip kissed Dalton, who looked as beautiful and as young as she did when he first met her. "I have an idea. Since they'll all be converging on us for dinner, why don't we have a little flying time? Just the two of us, before they all arrive. You know as well as I that the skies will be darkened with all of them up there."

"I'd very much love that."

The two of them made their way to the yard. They had been looking at every area to make sure that the house and yard were ready. Button was there as well, happy to have the children all home again, just as she was every year.

Did you tell Button about the three new babies that are coming? She usually has more time with them than we do.

She does not. It's you that has all the time. Last year you slept in the nursery with the children. I think you had more fun with their toys than they did. They took to the skies. Kip loved the way her dragon sparkled in the sunlight. *This is the way it should be. Don't you think? Children to have fun with. An open sky to enjoy, and money enough to take care of those that take care of us. I don't think that anything could be any better.*

He thought about his job, principle of the middle school for decades now. It was his favorite job he'd ever had, watching youngsters learning and creating in an environment that was safe and fun.

I agree.

They had nine biological children. Plus, two daughters and two sons that they had adopted so long ago now. The grandchildren were coming up on the big number twenty. Great grandchildren and beyond were too many to count. But they loved them all the same. They did have a special place in their hearts for Brody and Ryan; they were their first sons, the ones that they'd learned so much from.

The children that they had were a mixture of humans and dragons—seven sons and two daughters. Kip would admit that he had more fun with his sons when they came over, but he loved his daughters more than he did food. And that was saying a great deal.

Pop-pop was the name that all of them called him, children and grand alike. They called Dalton Momma, and GG Maw for the great grandchildren. They had a wonderfully full life, and would pull out pictures of them all when asked about them. Smiling, he saw Button come to him when they landed on the mountain top. He'd had it in his mind to make love to Dalton, but the children were arriving, Button told them. There was no time.

"You were remiss in not telling me about the new ones, my lord. There are three of your grandchildren having babes of their own again, and I was not aware of it. Whatever shall I do with you?" He laughed when she gave him a stern look. "I should have known too. Now I have no special gift for them."

I doubt that is true, Button. You have been as bad as Lady Dalton, stashing away gifts so that you'd always be prepared should any of them drop by. She laughed with him. *Who is it that has come? Which son?*

"Lord Brody, my lord. His wife, she is large with another child too." He said that he'd known that. "Yes, well, did you know that she carries twins?"

"Nay, I did not. Thank you for that, Button."

It was time for them to go back to the house, but he had one more thing to do. When they were both human again, dressed in their most comfy clothing to play with them all, he kissed Dalton on the mouth and then bent to one knee. "My lovely bride of all these decades, I love you more today than I did yesterday, and will love you even more on the morrow. You are my life, my heart, and my love. Dalton Newton, you have given all of this to me, and I cannot find the words that would show that to you."

"You are such a sap, my love." He kissed her again, putting the diamond bracelet around her wrist. "It's beautiful. But what will happen to it should I have to shift? I would hate for it to be broken."

"It has a few links around it that will stretch when you shift. There is a small tracker made into it so that you can find it when it may get lost." She kissed him again, and he felt like he owned the world. "I so very much love you."

Making their way back to the yard as humans, the bracelet shone as brightly as her scales did as her dragon. All of their children had arrived while they'd been on the mountain top. Their sons decided it was the perfect time to get some flying in with their dear old dad. Kip wasn't sure that he liked being called old—he looked as young as they did—but he took to the skies with them. He was so happy now that Brody and Ryan had received the dragons from his sister and father. It was fitting, he thought, for them to be dragons with the rest of their family.

Dalton was already fussing over the new babies, as well as the older children. He saw the others, Danburn included, pulling into the drive when they were above them.

Family. There wasn't a thing in the world that meant more to him. It was the circle of life, and while he had done his best to make sure that his circle was wide, he knew that his family was only a drop in the hat compared to all the families of the world. Still, Kip thought that he had the best.

The town was very prosperous now. There was not only a fully operating hospital, but they had specialists in all manner of skills there. The clinic was open too. All the shifters mostly used it, but when there was an emergency, they were as welcome at the hospital as any other person was.

They had a department store like none other. It was a place to get local goods, from hand carved toys to clothing for both women and men. In addition to that, there was a pharmacy and a large ice cream shop. Carmine had been running it, giving away more ice cream than she sold since she'd gotten her dragon—she carried a dragon whose human had decided that it no longer wished to be around. It suited her, having an older dragon, as she had been an old soul even as a child. Kip was very proud of the way the two of them had finally come together.

Elissa, Danburn's mother, had left them one day and had yet to return. Danburn thought that his mother would come back someday, but Kip didn't think so. Elissa had been a great role model for all the women in the family, and had loved them all like she did the boys, as she called them, that Danburn had befriended so long ago.

"Look at you, Kip. My goodness, you look like you've gotten a peek at all the presents that have been stashed in the house." Hugging Danburn, he was happy that all those centuries ago his father had saved him. "I was thinking that next year we'd have a couple of roasted hogs, and invite the neighborhood too."

"Beat you to it, my good man. Or Dalton did. She's invited all the town up to have something to eat, and for the fireworks tonight." Danburn pouted. He was really good at it. But Kip refrained from telling him he looked like his youngest granddaughter when he did it. "You're the one that suggested the fireworks, and I do think that is going to be the highlight of the night."

"You think so? You should have told me, Kip. Any and all of us would have chipped in on this. You've gone all out this year." Kip reminded him that he did have Thanksgiving for all of them. "Yes, but this is so much more fun. You have a pool the size of my lake, all the treats for the children. I am glad that you have let us help out with the scholarships that are awarded every year."

They all put their money together, thousands of dollars, and gave ten high school seniors a full scholarship to any college they could get into. That had been Kendrick's idea. She had wanted to go to college when she'd been younger, but it never panned out for her. Now she had three degrees, Kip thought, and was working on the fourth.

Dana found him near the chest freezer handing out ice cream cones to anyone that wanted one. He and his mate had been busy with all sorts of projects over the years. Mostly they were for children that had been made orphans by one accident or another. Their house looked like it had a revolving door all the time. Kip wasn't sure, but he'd bet that over the years they had rescued a thousand children and helped them out.

Griffith now spent some of his time here in this realm, and a great deal of time in the faerie world. He was king of them now, his mate the queen. Kassian had retired some time ago, and now ran a daycare center on this side of her realm. The children begged to be there because of how great Kassian was with them. Also, the horde of faeries wasn't too bad either. He watched her as she played with the children while showing them how not to pick a flower.

Rette had been mayor off and on for decades. Every time he would think about retiring, he'd be pushed back into the job again and again. He was good at it. And he was much better at asking for help than he had been. That was why they had the lowest unemployment rate in all the country, as well as an extremely low crime rate. It was a peaceful, safe town.

Hanson and Quinn were doing great. The restaurant was doing very well. Quinn even brought in a few kids from the local college so they could learn some of the trade secrets of running or even working in a place like hers. Du—David—a man that had been a dragon watcher whose dragon had died long before any of the children had been born, was still around too, loving that all the children from everyone in the families called him Uncle Du. He still thought it was his job to take care of Quinn when she wasn't with Hanson.

The women, all very strong in their own right, were the ones that kept everyone happy. Even if they had to come down on someone that was acting up, as Dalton called it, they were also quick to make sure that they got on the right path again. If not— Well, if they didn't, they were thrown in the jail cell, the only place in the entire town that wasn't cheerful, Kip thought, and had a better outlook on what they were to do from now on.

Dalton had been running the police station for what seemed like forever. She was good at her job, and didn't get taken advantage of at all. Even bigger men, some that weren't familiar with her, would soon realize their mistake if they thought her a pushover. Dalton carried a gun, and knew just how to make it sing, as she called it. Few came back to her once she set them straight, and most thanked her for the path that she'd put them on. Kip never asked what was in the jail cell that would have a person changing so quickly, but whatever it was, he was sure that he didn't want to spend any time there either.

Holding two of the ice creams in his hand, Kip went in search of Dalton. He should have known that she'd be in the thick of things. She was rocking two of the children and talking to their daughters at the same time. The conversation had something to do with an upcoming party, and he steered clear of it. Handing off the ice cream, he found Danburn sitting in one of the many chairs that had been brought out for the occasion.

~*~

Danburn took the drink that one of the faeries had bought to him and put his melting ice cream in it. They had one for Kip too when he joined him. He waited, knowing that soon enough the others would join them too. It was something that they did every year—figure out ways to keep the young here and to make sure that everyone had a job that they could do. When they were all six together, he thought about how he loved these men just as if they were really his blood brothers. They had come through so much, and had become better men and better friends to each other. He was just the same Danburn he'd always been.

"What are you thinking about?" Danburn was startled out of his thoughts by Hanson. "Carmine told me to tell you that you need to loosen up. Without you then none of us would be here. What has her saying that? If you don't mind me asking, what has you looking so blue?"

"I do mind, but I'll tell you anyway. And tell your daughter to mind her own business." They both laughed as the rest of them talked about this and that. "I was just thinking how I've not changed at all. Gone through what you men have to come to be what you are today."

"Seriously?" Danburn told him he was. "Christ, man, do you remember us coming to you when we needed a safe haven? The things your mother and father did for us? I'd like to point out that I'd be dead without them holding my hand when I needed it."

"I didn't have to do anything to get them to love you as much as I already did. All of you, you've been through so much and have come out winners each time. Me? I just had the power to build a castle and provide a place for you to live when you needed it." Hanson told the others what was being said. All of them looked at him like he had two heads. "Listen, you guys are good friends, but you would have come out all right, even if I'd not been there with you."

"No we wouldn't have." Danburn looked at Rette when he spoke. "I would never have found Cassie without you. Not to mention, without your support and understanding, I think that I would have died with my mother and not ever have been as happy as I am at this moment."

"As for me," Hanson said. "Do you think that I would have ever been able to have fallen in love with Cassie? She wouldn't have been here for me to find had you not given her a job and your friendship. Also, and this is a big one, you've given each and every one of us the confidence that we so sorely needed. Simply because you have it." Danburn said he wasn't so sure about that. "I am. Ask any of the others and they'll tell you too."

"I agree with you, Danburn. You're nothing but a slob

that not one of us like." They all laughed with Dana when he spoke again. "You're our best friend, Danburn. I hope you know that. You're also the man who helped us when we thought nothing could. Not just with our families, but you also shared yours with us. Without that, I don't think that I would have understood what a good relationship was. Certainly not a loving one. We all looked up to you. That's the simple truth."

Griff laughed before he said anything. "All I can think about is the story you told us about Kendrick when you first met her. I swear to you, Danburn, I wish I could have been here when you were trying to make her do what you thought that she should." Danburn said he might have not made it either had it not been for Noah. "Yes, that man is a treasure. I swear, he must be telling your oldest how much trouble you were all the time."

"Christ, I hope not. I always knew I'd fucked up when he called me sir or my lord. And if he said them both in the same sentence, I knew I wasn't going to get anything that I wanted." Danburn looked at Kendrick. "To think that I was so angry with her, and she only had to sock me in the nose to get my attention."

Kip sat there for a long time, not saying anything until the others drifted away or were called away by their family. He thought that of all his friends, Kip was the one that he liked the most. He had been the most laid back man since his family was taken to task than any of the others. He also had a heart of gold. A man that he could and did talk with when he needed to.

"When I was living at home, your father came to see my parents. It wasn't a social call or anything like that. Lord Fletcher pounded on the door with his fist and splintered the front door like it was made of cardboard. When he was turned away, he shoved the butler back then out of the way, and yelled at the top of his lungs for my father." Danburn remembered this story. It was one of his favorites, and the one that gave him nightmares whenever he thought about it. "My father came down the stairs, screaming about it being his house and that Fletcher wasn't welcome there. I was locked in the cell under the stairs, but I could hear them well enough."

"Dad told me about that day. And that when he broke you out of the cell, you'd lost so much weight that he feared for your life." Kip nodded and watched the children playing. "You stayed with us for over a month that time."

"I would have gladly spent my life with you had it not been for my sister." Danburn remembered that too. Bethany had called to the dragon council and told them that his dad had taken Kip against his will. Nothing could have been further from the truth. "When they arrived at the house, we were just having dinner. I was still very thin, but I was mending. I'll never forget what your father said to mine."

"He said that if anything more happened to you that he'd come after him. Dad also told them that it wasn't an idle threat. I remember for the rest of the summer, you got better and were happier than I ever remember you being." Kip nodded. "Then it all fell apart."

"Yes. I spent the next six months at your house. My legs were both broken, my shoulder too. I couldn't shift either, because I was so weak at the time." Danburn wanted to change the subject, and nearly did when Kip spoke again. "Your father taught me something that fall. He taught me that not all parents were like mine. Nor like yours. He said there were good, bad, and in between. He told me too that someday I'd meet a woman that would be nothing like anyone I'd ever met before, and she would love me so strongly and show me how to love that I'd be as happy as he was with his own mate. Then he told me that I had the opportunity to make a decision right then on what sort of parent that I wanted to be. Good, bad, or in-between. He said that good parents loved their children above all else. That's what he did for you. Bad parents were mine at the time. In between parents were as indifferent about their children as they could be, and were the worst kind of parents. They neither cared nor didn't care enough about them to give two shakes if they were happy, healthy, or sick. He told me that he'd rather I was a bad parent than an indifferent one. But he hoped that I would be the good kind."

"You are. You know that, don't you?" Kip nodded and smiled at him. "Kip, I honestly don't know what I'd have done all my life if not for you. For the same reasons too. You showed me that bad doesn't breed bad. Nor does good breed good. It really is as my father told you. You must make that decision and stick to it. I'm so very honored every day that you were my very best of friends."

"I will be forever too."

Danburn sat with Kip for another hour or so. Family came and went. They would enjoy their company for a while before they too moved on. Life was like that, Danburn thought. People would come in and out of their lives forever. It was the ones that made the biggest impression on their hearts that they'd love.

By the time dinner was ready to eat, they were all there. All six families, and their families as well. Something that Danburn had been working on since the last get together was ready to be shown too. Pulling out the projector as well as the camera that would show them, Danburn showed all the pictures of them throughout the years. Even he got teary eyed at a great many of them.

He and Kendrick walked home after everyone started

leaving. They'd be together for the next week, the families would, and he was going to enjoy every bit of it. Wrapping his arm around his wife, he entered the house and was met by his new butler, Phillip—new as in he'd been working for them for the past several decades.

"You have a guest, my lord, as I'm sure you know." As Phillip handed a shirt and tie to him, he waited with his hand out for his T-shirt.

"We have a guest? The children?" Phillip huffed but didn't say anything more. "Then perhaps you'll tell me why I'm getting dressed up. Are we having a party?"

"Yes. A party. In your mother's honor. It's her birthday. She has come a long way only to be greeted by myself—"

If Phillip spoke any more, Danburn didn't hear it. His mother was there.

"Mother?" She hugged him after she was finished hugging Kendrick. "Why didn't you tell me you were coming? I would have avoided Phillip's anger at me and been here to meet you."

"What fun would that have been?" Danburn hugged her again as Kendrick told him how she had wanted it to be a surprise. "I was so glad that I could pull one over on you, Danburn. You are very hard to surprise with all your snooping around."

"I do not snoop." Kendrick told him that she'd get some tea for them, and held his mom again. "I'm so glad that you're here this year. Everyone will be glad to see you."

"And I them. Tell me what I've missed." Danburn laughed and told her it was too much for one night. "Then I shall find out tomorrow what I've missed. Oh my son, it is so wonderful to be home again. I cannot wait to see the children too."

"They're all grown now, most of them anyway." She nodded and sipped her tea that Phillip brought in for them.

"I'm so glad you're here. It's like old times now. Everyone home and so much to see. I love you, Mom.

"And I love you, my dear boy. I do hope you got me something." He laughed as Phillip and the rest of the staff started bringing out gifts for her. "Goodness, Danburn. What did I do to deserve all this?"

"You've been gone far too long, and I've saved them for you."

She laughed as Kendrick sat by him. After kissing her on the cheek, he talked to his mom. There was a great deal to catch up on, and he couldn't wait to see the faces of the others when they found out she was home. For good, he hoped.

Danburn felt as if his life was as full as he could get it. Family and friends were really all he needed, and they were here with him now. Life, he decided, was perfect.

Before You Go...

HELP AN AUTHOR

write a review

THANK YOU!

Share your voice and help guide other readers to these wonderful books. Even if it's only a line or two your reviews help readers discover the author's books so they can continue creating stories that you'll love. Login to your favorite retailer and leave a review. Thank you.

Kathi Barton, winner of the Pinnacle Book Achievement award as well as a best-selling author on Amazon and All Romance books, lives in Nashport, Ohio with her husband Paul. When not creating new worlds and romance, Kathi and her husband enjoy camping and going to auctions. She can also be seen at county fairs with her husband who is an artist and potter.

Her muse, a cross between Jimmy Stewart and Hugh Jackman, brings her stories to life for her readers in a way that has them coming back time and again for more. Her favorite genre is paranormal romance with a great deal of spice. You can visit Kathi online and drop her an email if you'd like. She loves hearing from her fans. aaronskiss@gmail.com.

Follow Kathi on her blog: http://kathisbartonauthor. blogspot.com/

www.ingramcontent.com/pod-product-compliance
Lightning Source LLC
Chambersburg PA
CBHW030224180626
46810CB00008B/2955